AMERICAN YOUTH

AMERICAN YOUTH

Phil LaMarche

SCEPTRE

Copyright © 2007 by Philip LaMarche

First published in the United States by Random House

First published in Great Britain in 2007 by Hodder & Stoughton
A division of Hodder Headline

Extract from *All the Pretty Horses* by Cormac McCarthy © 1993
reproduced by kind permission of Macmillan, London, UK.

A Sceptre Book

1

A CIP catalogue record for this title is available from the British Library

ISBN 978 0 340 93803 4

Printed and bound by Mackays of Chatham Ltd, Chatham, Kent

Hodder Headline's policy is to use papers that are natural, renewable
and recyclable products and made from wood grown in sustainable
forests. The logging and manufacturing processes are expected to
conform to the environmental regulations of the country of origin.

Hodder & Stoughton Ltd
A division of Hodder Headline
338 Euston Road
London NW1 3BH

For William Hanson,
1977–2005

Scars have the strange power to remind
us that our past is real.

—CORMAC MCCARTHY,
All the Pretty Horses

AMERICAN YOUTH

1

The two boys walked the high ridge at the center of the wood road, avoiding the muddy ruts along the sides. Loggers had powered their hulking machines along the makeshift pathways—the huge skidder tires clawing deep cuts into the soft earth. The men had taken the timber of any value and only the undesirable trees remained: the young, the mangled and twisted, the rotten and sick. The boys made their way through the difficult clutter of leftover branches that now thatched the forest floor. The sun broke the sparse canopy and beat on their sweating necks.

Terry caught a toe on the cut end of an exposed root and stumbled into several lurching steps. His backpack rattled.

The other boy sidestepped the splintered butt of wood and quickly tiptoed around a small birch stump. Terry stood a head taller than the boy and he was half again as broad, but he wore his body like an oversize suit. The boy was still small and nimble, but he wasn't happy about it. He looked at Terry's body and he wanted one of his own. Terry's neck and arms were thick like a man's. The backpack looked like a child's toy, dangling between his broad shoulders.

Terry tripped again. "Cocksucker," he said. He hopped the rut at the side of the path and took a seat on a broad stump. The cut wood was still pale and creamy. White sawdust clung to the dead leaves on the ground like early snow. Terry bent over his knees and clutched the laces of his work boot. He wore them untied and loose, as was the fashion in their school for boots and high-tops. Now he straightened his leg and leaned back, pulling the boot tight. He bow-tied the laces and set to his other foot.

The boy eyed Terry's hands and forearms as he pulled. They were covered in coarse red hair that matched the color of his closely shorn scalp. The boy's arms were undefined. What hair he had on his body was blond and thin.

Terry grunted when he stood. He hopped back on the trail. The boy was six months his senior, but Terry's size earned him the lead through the maze of skid roads. When Terry wondered which way to proceed, the boy pointed knowingly from behind. He'd grown up hunting the Darling land with his father and uncle. But several years back, Mr. Darling had died and his children had sold the property to a developer. Within weeks, NO TRESPASSING signs surrounded the four hundred acres. Within months, the land had been subdivided and the town's zoning board confronted with plans for a handful of upscale housing developments.

In effect, the boys were trespassing, but there was no one around to catch them. When the economy had gone bad and stayed bad, the development stopped. The groaning cement trucks quit their runs in and out of the new neighborhoods. The swarms of subcontractors disappeared and the developer's Mercedes no longer made its rounds about town. It was rumored that the money from the recent logging contract was all he had left to fend off foreclosure.

The boys walked out into the clearing of Woodbury Heights, the last of the developer's projects. He'd pushed the road into the woods, paved it, and even managed to cut several of the prospective house lots before the recession settled in. Piles of soil and unearthed boulders now cluttered the landscape. Leafless trees lay prone, their roots reaching elliptically into the air. The deep black of the new pavement stood out from the mess of the rest of the scene.

The boys made their way to the culvert at the end of the road. The August sun hung heavily on the two and came back at them from the hot blacktop.

"You sure?" the boy said.

Terry nodded. He slid his arms out of the backpack and pulled out three glass bottles.

"How you know?"

"My brother," Terry told him. "Two parts gas, one part oil." He took out three socks and tied knots in them. He soaked the socks with the mixture in the bottles and stuffed a knot through each open bottleneck. Then he went to the side of the road and wiped his hands on the tall grass.

When he returned, he took up one of the bottles, held a lighter to the sock, and heaved the cocktail. It crashed and set a good portion of pavement afire.

"See," Terry said. "Told you."

The boy smiled. "No shit," he said.

They watched the fire slowly subside.

Terry lit and tossed a second. Again the pavement burned.

"Let me," the boy said.

Terry handed him the last of the three bottles and the boy held it, his arm cocked and ready. Terry thumbed the lighter and touched it to the sock. The boy waited for the flame to catch, crow-hopped a quick three steps, and overhanded the bottle. It reminded him of some second-rate firework, the trajectory neither high nor fast. When it crashed down, the flames spilled across the tarmac and waved in the air. The boy stared at the fire, a dumb smile on his soft face.

A jab in the ribs brought him around quickly. Terry pointed a thumb down the road. His head was cocked, an ear in the direction of his hand. His eyes looked at the sky. The boy heard it too, an engine in low gear, climbing the hill. Terry turned and sprinted. The boy chased after him but couldn't keep up. With the sound of the engine growing closer, Terry didn't try to make it to the trail they'd come on. Instead he bolted over the shoulder of the road, through the underbrush, and into the woods. The boy followed.

With the broad hardwoods gone, the hiding wasn't good. Terry sprawled behind a fir sapling and the boy crouched behind a good-size stump. He panted, catching his breath. When he saw the police cruiser, his chest froze and he could hardly get more than a quick gasp. He looked back at Terry.

"Think it's burning?" the boy said.

Terry shrugged. "Come on," he said, once the cruiser had passed. He jumped to his feet and waved for the boy to follow.

"I don't think we should move."

"No way," Terry said, as he turned and lumbered into the woods. The boy looked back at the road. He heard Terry crashing through the brush and dead leaves behind him. He turned and ran after his friend. He didn't want to be alone.

Though Terry was a more powerful sprinter, his size worked against him over a longer distance and the boy overtook him.

"Where you going?" said the boy.

Terry pointed in the direction he was running.

The boy shook his head and motioned off to his right.

Terry nodded and followed.

When the two could run no farther, they stopped and rested, their torsos bent, hands heavy on their knees.

"Duncan?" the boy said.

Terry shrugged.

"I hope it was Duncan."

"Me too."

"Don't tell."

"Don't tell me not to tell. Christ," Terry said.

The boy looked down and then away.

"Besides," Terry told him, "I'm the one reeks of gas." He reached down and wiped his hands on the leaves of a small tree.

They walked until they reached Sandy Creek, the first development to go up on the Darling property. Prior to the building and landscaping, it had been a sandpit where teenagers rallied dirt bikes and hopped-up pickups. Where teenagers and twenty-somethings gathered around bonfires and drank beer until the police chased them out. Terry and the boy had hunted bullfrogs at the water holes there. When they couldn't catch them, they threw stones.

Now it was Sandy Creek, but in the heat of summer, the creek was more of a bog, and it plagued the new neighborhood with mosquitoes. The local carpenters and handymen had turned a good profit screening in the expansive porches of the new homes. On the road, the boy couldn't help noticing how different the subdivision was from the rest of the town. The uniform homes rose like tiered gunships from the ground, sitting nearly on top of one another—their grand picture windows looked out on other grand picture windows. The lawns were flat and cropped like crew cuts. The trees were planted. The gardens didn't bear produce.

At the end of the Sandy Creek road, the two boys stopped. Terry lived in one direction and the boy in the other.

"Want to come over?" Terry said.

The boy shook his head, unwilling to chance another encounter with Terry's two older brothers. They had a routine called the Daily Beating, and although the name implied a schedule, they simply pounced on Terry when the feeling struck them. During the boy's last visit, they included him in a new game they called Help Him—He's Drowning. One brother grabbed the boy by the back of the neck and dunked his head up and down in their above-ground pool. The other stood on the patio, pointing and shouting, "Help him—he's drowning! For the love of God, someone help!"

After hacking out the chlorinated water, hunkered on his hands and knees, the boy walked all the way home in his dripping swimsuit.

"No thanks," he told Terry.

Terry paused for a moment but the boy didn't extend an invitation.

"See you," Terry said.

"Yeah," said the boy.

When Terry was out of sight, the boy went back into Sandy Creek. He walked to the elaborate entryway of one of the large homes. It was hardly dusk, but the chandelier over the door was already lit. He'd ditched Terry because he knew his chances of getting invited inside were greater without him. Terry had fought Kevin Dennison earlier in the summer and fattened his lip. The boy pushed the doorbell and heard the elegant chime inside. He heard footsteps approaching and the door opened.

"Theodore," Mrs. Dennison said. She smiled and her eyes squinted. "How are you?"

The boy hated being called Theodore but he smiled back. "Fine," he said. "You?"

"Not bad," she said. Mrs. Dennison was young. Young to have kids his age, the boy thought. She was slender and her short dark hair looked shiny and soft to the touch. "Ready for school?"

He shook his head.

She smiled. "High school already. I can hardly believe it," she said. "Are you nervous?"

"Nah," he said.

"Don't tell him I said so, but I think Kevin is."

He smiled. "Kevin and Bobby here?"

"They're with their father," she told him.

He nodded. He knew the Dennisons were separated. He knew Mr. Dennison already had a girlfriend.

"Why don't you come by tomorrow," she said. "I'll tell them you were here."

"All right—have a good night."

"You too, Theodore." She smiled and retreated back inside the house.

He spun about, hopped down the stairs, and walked across the brick sidewalk to the road. When he turned, he balked at the sight of Terry, standing at the corner where they had parted. Terry had a cigarette. The boy knew the way he tried to hide it—his hand cupped around the butt, arm hanging casually at his side. Terry looked at the boy, took a drag, and left for the second time. An ill feeling settled inside the boy. He'd been caught in the midst of his defection, and worse, Terry had predicted the betrayal.

The boy scuffed his shoe hard across the pavement. He picked up a rock and hurled it at a real estate sign in front of a home. It struck loud and metallic. He winced and quickly looked around for any witnesses. The flash of fear overwhelmed the feeling he'd had upon seeing Terry—upon seeing Terry see him. He jogged to the end of the Sandy Creek road, but Terry was gone. The boy stood for a moment at the intersection before he turned and headed home.

As he walked, the din of evening crickets poured in from the surrounding woods. The pavement was old and cracked at the edges. The sand the town spread for traction in winter collected in small dunes in the ditch. Trees grew close at the sides and reached over the road. Some bore scars from accidents and run-ins with snowplows. Here and there a beer can littered the ditch, sometimes a hubcap or paper coffee cup.

Before the boy got to the Humphreys' house, he bent over and fisted two good-size stones. The Humphreys always had one mongrel dog or another that came to snarl at the foot traffic that passed. Every couple years the dogs were run down by cars and replaced. The boy passed in front of their home, but the dog didn't show. A barn stood on the back corner of their property and an old pony, round-bellied and sway-backed, wandered a corral back there. The boy remembered sneaking through the woods to throw rocks at the horse and watch it twitch and buck. He passed out of sight of the Humphreys' and dropped the two stones.

When he came around the bend to his house, he saw the real estate sign on his lawn. It was only two months old and it still caught his eye. His father had sold life insurance until the recession whittled away his commissions.

Earlier that summer, he found better work, but far off—in Pennsylvania. The boy's mother had fought the decision but her salary as a schoolteacher wouldn't cover the bills and there was little she could do but concede. The father moved into an efficiency, eight hours south, while the boy and his mother stayed home—the father hopeful for its sale, the mother for a change in the economy.

The boy walked across the mouth of the driveway and down the edge of the lawn. He eyed the front of the house and listened for coming cars. When all seemed clear he bent over and wrenched the sign back and forth, loosening the soil's grip on it. After that bit of handiwork, the sign came out easily.

Clods of dirt still clung to its legs. With a hand on the top two corners, he jogged to the opposite side of the road, raised the sign above his head, and heaved it into the ditch for the third time. On each occasion, the real estate agent would track it down, skewer it back in the lawn, and curse the local teenage hooligans. It was a small delight for the boy, and he knew he would keep at it until he was caught.

2

———————

Despite the Dennisons' air-conditioning and swimming pool, the three boys panted away the following afternoon at the boy's home. Kevin and Bobby wanted soda, but there was none. They wanted to watch cable television, but the only box on the top of the television had two rabbit-ear antennae protruding from it.

"You don't have crap to do," Bobby said. He was short and squat with a thick neck, like his older brother and father.

The boy shrugged. Bobby always complained that there wasn't anything to do.

"He has a gun," Kevin said.

"Bull," Bobby said.

"He does."

"Show us," Bobby said. "It's probably just a BB gun."

"I have two," the boy told them.

"Prove it," Bobby said.

"What kinds?" said Kevin.

"A twelve-gauge," the boy told them. "And a twenty-two."

"Let's see the twelve-gauge," Kevin said.

The boy shook his head. The shotgun was old, a hand-me-down from his uncle. He was afraid they would focus on the gun's nicks and scratches, or the way the pump action was worn and loose.

"He's bull," Bobby said. "That's why he won't."

The boy looked out the window and saw his mother working in the backyard. "I'll show you my twenty-two," he said.

"That's a stupid gun," Bobby said.

"Shut up," Kevin told his brother.

The boy shook his head. The gun wasn't stupid. His .22 was the only new firearm in the house—the others had been in the family for years: the 30-06 under the couch in the living room, the .300 Savage and the bolt-action 20-gauge in a closet in the basement, the shotgun under his father's bed.

He led the brothers to the china cabinet in the dining room. He reached underneath.

"Why here?" Kevin asked him.

"For the crows," he said.

Kevin looked confused.

"They wake him up some mornings," the boy said. "He

lets me shoot them. Out the window." He glanced over his shoulder at the window that looked out on the backyard.

"That's awesome," Kevin said.

The boy didn't mention that he had yet to fire a single shot. Every time he opened the window, the crows scattered in the air. And he knew better than to go firing off a volley at the airborne birds—there were houses back there beyond the woods, and though a small caliber, a .22 could send a bullet over a mile.

He drew the gun out by the stock and cradled it.

"It's a Remington," he said. He pointed the barrel at the floor and walked the Dennisons through the parts he knew. The brothers stared, and for a moment, they listened patiently.

"Let me hold it," Bobby said.

The boy pointed the barrel at the ceiling and handed him the gun. Bobby seemed surprised at how heavy it was. He smiled and leveled it at his brother.

"Bam," he said. "You're dead."

The boy grabbed the barrel and wrenched the gun away from him.

"Never do that," he said.

"What?"

"Point it."

"It's not loaded," Bobby said. "That's stupid."

"You're stupid," the boy said. He pulled out a drawer in the cabinet and removed a small box. "These are the bullets." He fingered open the box and removed one for them to see. Kevin held out his hand and the boy dropped it into his palm. The two brothers bent their necks to study the round.

"It's puny," Bobby said.

"Show us how to put it in." Kevin held the bullet back in the boy's direction.

"There," he told Kevin, pointing to the chamber. "And close this." He slid the bolt closed and locked it down.

"No," Kevin said. "For real."

The boy shook his head.

"Why?" Bobby said.

"We're inside."

"Come on," Kevin said. "Do it."

"Show us," Bobby said.

The boy looked at them. Their eyes seemed so eager, so captivated. He held out his hand and Kevin returned the bullet to his palm. He took a breath and drew back the action. He looked at Kevin and Bobby as if to say, *Like this,* and let the bullet into chamber. He fisted the ball on the end of the bolt, slid it forward, and locked it down. It felt beautiful—the slide and clack of steel coupling with steel. He exhaled and looked at them. They smiled. Bobby rocked back and forth from one foot to another.

A noise outside jarred the boy and he walked to the window. His mother wasn't in the backyard. He looked nervously from the .22 to the Dennisons. He knew that showing it off would land him in a shit storm of trouble. He bent over and slid it back under the cabinet.

He moved quickly to the window in the adjacent room and was relieved to find her in the side yard. She was sweeping up the sand on the side of the road. With a snow shovel she lifted piles of it into a wheelbarrow. His mother was small but strong. When she got ahold of him, he was helpless in her hard hands. She could shake him like a rag doll. His breathing calmed at the sight of her, but he felt guilty, watching her work. He knew he should be helping.

As he turned from the window, he flinched at the concussion of the loud clap in the house. He was puzzled only for an instant. It was different inside, but still he knew the noise. His fists clenched and his jaw bore down on his teeth until it felt as though they might give. He was sure his father would find out, would take his gun and get furious and silent for days. He wondered if he could hide it, some small cavity in the Sheetrock or molding. Maybe the shot went through the floor, the hole hidden by the nap of the carpet, the bullet lost in the dark basement.

As the boy breached the doorway to the room and saw Bobby on his back, the anger left him. His lungs stammered, unable to commit to the next breath that his body so needed. He looked at Kevin. Kevin was crying.

"My ears," Kevin said.

"What?"

"My ears," he said. "I can't hear."

"What happened?"

"He wanted it and I wasn't done. He pulled it." Kevin shoved the gun back at the boy and left the room. The boy walked toward Bobby. A small bubble of spit rose from Bobby's lips and burst. His eyes blinked, but other than that he didn't move. The boy moved closer and Bobby's eyes found him. There was a confusion in his face, like a dog hearing a new sound. The boy nearly jumped when Bobby moved. His hand came up and brushed at the small bloody spot on his chest like it was an itch or some crumbs. Then his arm stopped and lay still again. The spot on Bobby's chest was close to his left nipple. With his hand over it, he looked ready for the national anthem or the Pledge of Allegiance.

The boy looked down at the .22. He drew back the bolt and held out his hand to catch the spent shell. He held it to his nose and smelled the sulfurous mouth. He pocketed the casing, closed the action, and put the gun back under the cabinet. He turned and crouched, both feet under him, his elbows on his knees. He watched Bobby closely, the small movements here and there. Bobby stared at the ceiling.

The boy turned when he heard a noise behind him, and he was startled to see his mother. His body seized with the fear of a forthcoming punishment, but she didn't come for him. She didn't scream. Without so much as acknowledging the boy's presence, she walked quickly over and fell to her knees beside Bobby.

"Call an ambulance," she said. He stood alone behind her and watched. She took Bobby's wrist in her hand. She put her ear to his mouth. She pinched Bobby's nose and put her lips to his. She exhaled, paused, and exhaled again. She kneeled upright, put one hand atop the other, and pumped on Bobby's chest. She turned her hands over and looked at them. One had a thick sheen of blood. She looked from her hand to the boy behind her. "Go, goddammit."

He went to the next room and dialed the three numbers. He did his best to explain what had happened.

"Is he breathing?" the voice on the other end asked.

"A little, maybe," he said. "I don't know."

"I have some people on the way now, but I need to ask you a few more questions."

"Fine," he said.

The dispatcher proceeded and he answered the best he could but he was distracted by the sounds from the neighboring room. He stretched the cord and took the receiver away from his ear so that he could peer around the doorjamb. His mother sat up and wiped her hands on the legs of her jeans. She slowly shook her head. Her shoulders jumped twice and she brought a hand to her face. After a moment, she leaned over Bobby and pushed his bangs from his forehead. She ran her fingers through his hair and parted it to the side. She whispered something but the boy could hear only the soft outline of her voice. She patted his hair in place and slowly drew her hands back along his cheeks. She bent again to press her mouth to Bobby's and the boy felt a pang as witness to this. He felt separate. He felt alone and he quickly looked away.

When the ambulance arrived, he put the phone down on the counter and went to the door. Two men and a woman moved quickly up the sidewalk carrying heavy shoulder bags. The boy held the door open for them and pointed to the dining room but they stopped on the front stairs. The man in front asked him what had happened. The boy told him that Bobby had been shot.

"Who did it?" the man asked him.

"His brother."

"Where is he now?"

The boy shrugged. "Bobby's right in here. He needs help." He couldn't understand their hesitation.

"Where's the kid with the gun?" the man said. But before the boy could answer, the woman suddenly stepped forward and shouldered the man aside.

"Where is he?" she said to the boy, her head bent down to him. "The hurt one?"

The boy pointed and she walked past him.

"Wait," the man shouted after her. "There's a kid with a gun."

"He doesn't have the gun," the boy told him. "He left it."

The man shook his head and stepped through the doorway, the second man on his heels. The boy followed them in but stopped at the doorway of the dining room. The woman pushed his mother back from Bobby and handed her something for the blood on her hands. After feeling Bobby's wrist and neck and listening to his mouth, the first man placed a plastic mask over Bobby's face. He gave Bobby two blows and the second man set to pumping on his chest—much harder than his mother had. Bobby's head bucked. It looked terribly painful.

His mother took him hard by the wrist and pulled him out of the room. She had sweat on her brow. She took him to the couch in the other room and they both sat.

"What did you do?" she said.

"Mum, it wasn't me."

She didn't say anything. She dipped her chin and looked hard at him.

"It wasn't," he told her. "It was Kevin."

"Tell me," she said. "Exactly."

He told her how he had showed them the gun, loaded it, and stuffed it back under the cabinet.

"You loaded it?" she said.

He nodded.

"Goddammit," she said. "You know better than that."

He started to speak, but he heard more sirens approaching. He lifted himself onto the arm of the couch and looked over his shoulder, out the window. There was a quick squeal of tires as the cruiser turned into the driveway. Almost immediately another cop car appeared and parked behind the first. The boy's breathing got away from him.

"Watch what you say," his mother said. He shook and began to cry. His mother locked a hard hand around his biceps and squeezed. "Theodore," she said. "You didn't load that gun. Understand?"

He looked at his mother.

"Do you understand me?"

He dropped his chin twice in agreement.

The officers banged at the door but they didn't wait. Duncan walked immediately to the boy and his mother, the other officer helped one of the EMTs wheel a gurney into the room where Bobby was. Duncan was tall with short gray hair and a matching mustache.

"Who can give me an idea of what happened here?" he said.

The boy slowly raised his hand as if he were in school, as if he had an answer he wasn't sure was right. He started his story again, and again he was interrupted.

"Wait," Duncan said, holding up a hand. "Where's Kevin now?"

"I don't know," the boy said.

"Shit," said Duncan. He picked up the radio that clung to his lapel and began talking into it. As he mumbled into the radio, the boy watched them wheel Bobby by. He wanted Bobby to smile and give him the thumbs-up, but Bobby didn't move. Two men maneuvered the gurney while a woman pumped a plastic ball that attached to Bobby's face with a clear mask.

"How long ago did he leave?" Duncan said.

The boy didn't know. It felt like days and seconds at the same time.

"He can't be far," the mother said. "It couldn't have been more than fifteen minutes."

"I need a description," Duncan said.

The boy and the mother pieced together some details.

"Varney," Duncan shouted.

"Talk to me," the other officer said as he walked into the room.

"We got a missing shooter, or possible shooter," Duncan said. "Take the unit and see if you can find him. Early teens, brown hair, five foot or so. Kevin Dennison. Lives on Sandy Creek. Head out there."

"Got you," Varney said. He left the room.

The boy heard the screen door bang shut.

"Possible shooter?" the mother said.

"I'm not here to make any decisions, Donna."

"It was an accident," she said. "Teddy just told you."

"It's not my job to determine that," Duncan told her. "I'm here to secure the scene and separate the witnesses, which seems to have already been done for me."

"You're going to separate us?"

"He's a minor so you have the right to stay with him."

"We can have a lawyer, right?" she said.

Duncan shook his head. "You don't get Miranda until we arrest you."

"What are you going to arrest him for?"

"The troopers and the attorney general will determine the charges," Duncan said.

"I don't think all this is necessary," she told him.

"In case you haven't noticed," Duncan said. "We got a shooting where the accused has fled the scene. Not to mention a missing weapon."

"It's under the cabinet," the boy said.

"Huh?" Duncan looked quickly at him.

The boy pointed toward the other room.

"Why is it there?"

"That's where it belongs."

"I see," Duncan said.

A voice began to squawk from the radio on his lapel and he stepped out of the room. The boy tried to listen to the exchange between Duncan and his radio, but the officer mumbled in a low tone and the voice from the radio was distorted and static-ridden.

"We got Kevin," Duncan said as he reentered the room. "And we've got an investigator on the way. You expecting Pete?"

"He's out of town," the mother said. "I'll call him when you leave."

Duncan shook his head. "Not if you want to stay with your boy. He's headed to the station."

"Do I have a minute?" she said.

"What for?"

She motioned at the dark stains on the legs of her pants.

"Go on," he said. After she left the room, he leaned in to the boy and spoke quietly: "This all has to go a certain way, no matter what happened. Understand?"

The boy nodded. He wanted to smile but he didn't. Something in him had changed. He couldn't say exactly what it was, but he felt different. It didn't feel like he was sitting on the couch, there in the room. It felt like he was somewhere inside his skull, watching the room through the windows of his eyes.

3

Waiting in the holding room reminded the boy of being in the doctor's office. Any minute the door could open, but the minutes kept passing and no one came. The fluorescent lights above them hummed and flickered. His chair squeaked whenever he shifted his weight.

"I'll handle this," his mother said.

"Ma," he whined.

"You have no idea what all's at stake here," she hissed in a whisper. "You let me do what I can." Her tone stopped his protest. He nodded and looked down at his clasped hands in his lap.

When the door finally opened, he flinched and his mother stood to greet the officer.

"Hello, Mrs. LeClare," he said, holding out a hand. "Trooper Thompson, Department of Major Crime." The two shook hands.

"Pleased to meet you," the mother said. "Well, not really." She faked a smile.

"I understand," he said. He reached toward the boy and they shook.

The boy was intimidated by the trooper. He looked young and he looked like a bruiser. His jaw was thick and square and covered in dark stubble. His left eyebrow was cut in two by a scar.

"I'll be working to determine what happened today," he said. "I apologize for my appearance." He rubbed his face. "I've been on all night—we're a bit short-staffed at the moment." He took a seat across from them. "I got most of the basics from Duncan," he said. "But there's a lot more to cover. Can I ask you this, Teddy—have you ever been in trouble before?"

"Of course not," his mother said.

"Mrs. LeClare, I need answers from Teddy right now. You'll have your chance later."

"Me?" she said.

"Of course. He's your son, it was your home, and you were the first on the scene," he said. "Now, Teddy, any trouble?"

"What kind?"

"Like this. With the law."

"Duncan picked us up one time, on the highway, on our bikes."

"Us?"

"Me and Terry," the boy said. "Terry Duvall. We were taking the shortcut to the Waterhouse, the convenience store."

"Anything else?" the trooper said.

The boy looked at his mother. Then he looked at the floor. "One time he picked us up hitching on the bypass."

"What?" the mother said.

The trooper held a hand up. "You can hide him for it later," he told her. "Let's just get through this." He let his hand down and looked back at the boy. He was fighting a smile. "You and Terry?"

The boy nodded.

"Where were you headed this time?"

The boy shrugged.

"How far you get?"

"Duncan was the only one to stop," the boy said.

"What did he do?"

"Took us home."

"Nice of him," the trooper said.

The boy nodded. "He even let us off about a hundred yards from our houses. So our folks wouldn't see us get out of the car."

The trooper smiled and shook his head. "I have to find a job in a town like this."

"Better hurry up," the mother said. "It isn't going to be small for long."

The trooper nodded. "A lot of changes, I'm sure," he said.

"You wouldn't believe it," she said.

"I'm a transplant myself," the trooper told her.

"I know it. The way you talk. You're from Boston. Moved here to raise your kids, I bet."

"Nail on the head," he said. "I'm impressed."

"I've been here a little while."

"Teddy, let's start yesterday, around this time," the trooper said. "What were you doing?"

"What's yesterday got to do with anything?"

"Mrs. LeClare, it's my job to collect a twenty-four-hour history of everyone involved. Now, will you let me do my job?"

"Please, go ahead."

He was about to start when she interrupted him again.

"You can call me Donna."

He nodded. "Teddy, yesterday, about this time—talk to me."

"Me and Terry," the boy said. "We were out in the woods."

"The dynamic duo strikes again."

"We weren't doing nothing wrong."

"I didn't say you were," he said. "In the woods. Anywhere in particular?"

The boy shrugged.

"What were you doing?" the trooper said.

"Nothing."

"Nowhere doing nothing," the trooper said. "Sounds a bit vague, doesn't it?"

"I said we were walking the trails in the woods."

"You know when I get vague answers?" the trooper said. "When someone's trying to hide something. What are you trying to hide, Teddy?"

"Nothing."

"You guys out hitching on the bypass again? Or worse? You two fighting with the Dennison boys somewhere?"

The boy realized he was only causing more trouble. "We were on the Darling place," he said. "Or what used to be."

"That doesn't mean anything to me," the trooper said.

"They were trespassing," the mother told him. "The land's posted."

"Why were you trespassing?" the trooper asked him.

"They just logged it. We wanted to see what it looked like."

"I can accept that," the trooper said. "See how much easier this is when you tell the truth?"

The boy nodded.

"There's no reason for all that land to be posted," the mother said.

"That's something you can take up with the owner," the trooper said. "Let's keep it rolling, Teddy."

He told the trooper about ditching Terry to see the Dennisons. Then he had to explain the fight that Terry had had with Kevin at the beginning of the summer. The trooper didn't seem to care much about it. He did want to know about the Dennisons.

"How would you describe them, as a family?" the trooper asked.

"Fine," said the boy. "Nice."

"Nothing you ever seen or heard made you question that?"

The boy shook his head.

"Nothing besides them being separated and him having a girlfriend half his age," the mother said.

Thompson nodded at her. "Violence?" he said to the boy. "Drugs or alcohol?"

"I hardly know them," the boy said. "They're pretty new here."

"Kevin?" said the trooper. "Ever hear him say anything about smoking a little pot or drinking a few beers?"

The boy shook his head.

"How about Kevin and Bobby? How did they get along?"

"Fine," said the boy.

"They fight much?"

"They argued some but I never saw them really fight."

"What did they argue about?"

"Stupid stuff. Brother stuff."

The trooper seemed satisfied and continued. The boy told him about the night after his stop at the Dennisons' and the following morning. The trooper seemed uninterested.

"Tell me about what happened after Kevin and Bobby arrived," the trooper said.

"They wanted to see my guns."

"Why?" the trooper said.

"They were bored."

"How did they go about asking to see the guns?"

"They said I didn't have anything to do. They said my house was boring. Mostly Bobby. Then Kevin told him about my guns and they wouldn't quit after that."

"How did Kevin know you had a gun?"

The boy shrugged. "It wasn't a big secret. I probably said it sometime."

"Then what?"

"Then I showed them."

"Can you explain that for me?"

"I took them to the dining room and pulled it out from under the cabinet," he said. "We kept it there because the crows bothered my dad sometimes."

"There's a season for crows," the mother said. "They both got a small-game license."

"I don't care about the crows," the trooper said. "Was the gun loaded when you took it from under the cabinet?"

"Of course not," the mother said. "What kind of people you think we are?"

The trooper waited until she finished. "Teddy?"

"It wasn't loaded," he said.

"How did you know it wasn't?"

"We never keep them loaded. But I knew it wasn't because the action was open and I could see the chamber was empty."

"Then what?"

"Bobby wanted to hold it so I handed it to him," the boy said. "But he pointed it at his brother so I took it back. I told him he was stupid."

"Why?"

"Because you're supposed to treat every gun like it's loaded. No matter what."

"How would you describe your experience with firearms?"

"My experience?"

"How much have you been around them? How much instruction have you had?"

"Dad taught me to shoot at what, Ma—six?"

She nodded.

"He and my uncle always taught me to be safe," he said. "I had to take the hunters' safety course to get my deer tags. I got the card at the house."

The trooper nodded. "And how would you describe the Dennisons' experience, before today?"

The boy shrugged. "Probably none."

"And you were aware of this?"

"I guess."

"So you took the gun back from Bobby," the trooper said. "Then what?"

"I showed them the bullets."

"Where were they?"

"In a drawer, in their box."

"Who handled the bullets?"

"I took them out and handed one to Kevin."

"How did you hold it?" the trooper said.

The boy shrugged. "What do you mean?"

"By the casing? By the tip?"

He shrugged again. "I don't know," he said.

The trooper reached down and pulled a round from his belt. He held it out toward the boy. "Could you show me?"

The boy hesitated but then reached up and took the bullet. "Like this, I guess." The pads of his thumb and index finger held the brass casing.

"Did you touch any other parts of it?" the trooper asked him. "The primer?"

"There's no primer on a twenty-two," he told the trooper. "It's rimfire."

"Did you touch any other part?"

"Maybe," he said. "When I put it back in the box."

"You're sounding a little vague again, Ted."

"How is he supposed to remember that?" the mother interrupted. "A boy was just shot."

The trooper held up an open hand in her direction. "You don't have to remind me what happened, Mrs. LeClare. Then what?" he said to the boy.

The boy shrugged.

"How did the firearm get loaded?"

"He knows better than to load a gun in the house," the mother said.

"Mrs. LeClare, I won't ask you again. Teddy, how did the firearm get loaded?"

The boy looked at his mother. He looked back to the trooper. He shrugged again.

"Teddy?"

"I don't know," he said. "I heard something. I thought it was my mom so I put the gun back under the cabinet. I couldn't see her in the backyard and I went to another window. Then I heard the gun go off and I ran back. Bobby was on the ground and Kevin had it. He said Bobby tried to take it from him. Then he made me take it. I took the casing out and put the gun back under the cabinet. That's when my mom came."

"So how did the gun get loaded?"

"I don't know," he said. "I guess one of them."

"I thought you said they didn't have any experience with guns," Thompson said. "How would they know how to load it?"

"I showed them, before."

"How did you show them?"

"I pointed to the chamber and told them that's where a bullet goes," he said. "Then I closed the bolt."

"Where's the empty casing now?"

The boy stood and reached into his front pocket. He came out with the empty shell and handed it over to the trooper. The trooper held up his hand for him to wait. He went into his pocket and came out with a handkerchief. He unfolded the fabric and held it open for the casing. The boy dropped it in and the trooper carefully set it to rest on the table before him.

"How come you took it?"

"Seemed important," he said.

"Can't argue with that," the trooper said. "I'm going to step out to get this bagged. Give me a minute." He took the handkerchief and left the room.

When the door closed, the boy spun to face his mother. "Ma?" he said.

She looked at the floor.

"Ma?" He was more insistent, near pleading.

"I don't know," she said. "Good Christ, I don't."

He was shaken by this change in her and he began to cry. When she saw him, she sat upright. She seemed to gather herself. She slid her chair closer and pulled him into an embrace. Her hand was warm and heavy on the back of his neck.

"Easy," she whispered. "Just breathe. You're crazy if you think I'd let them lay a hand on you."

He made sucking sounds as he tried to stifle the heaving in his chest. He remembered when two older neighborhood boys had chased him home, threatening to beat him up after an argument turned ugly. He sprinted to his yard and found his mother at work in the garden on her knees. Embarrassed as he was, he took shelter behind her and, without asking, she stood and faced off with the two teenagers. "There's two of you," she said. "Seems only fair there be two of us." She gripped a small spade like she meant to use it and the two boys departed, cursing under their breath.

Just as the boy was getting his breathing back under control, the trooper and Duncan stepped through the door.

"Could we have a moment with Theodore?" the trooper asked his mother.

"Alone?" she said.

He nodded. "Just a moment."

"No," she said. She shook her head.

"Donna?" Duncan said.

"We know this was an accident," the trooper told her. "Kevin's story and Teddy's corroborate that much."

"So what's the problem?" the mother asked him.

"There's some differences between their stories."

"Maybe Kevin's lying," the mother said.

The trooper paused. "Maybe," he said.

"Wouldn't you?" she asked him.

"Excuse me?" he said.

"If it was your brother?"

He looked at her for a moment. "I don't know, Mrs. LeClare."

"Donna," Duncan said. "It'll just be a minute."

"It's either me or a lawyer," she said. "Take your pick."

"Will you both sign statements?" Duncan asked her. "Attesting to what you've said?"

She nodded.

"All right," said the trooper. "Let's get that started. We're also going to need prints done and residue tests on your hands. And we're going to need your clothes, Teddy."

The boy looked at him.

"You didn't tell him to bring a change of clothes?" The trooper looked at Duncan.

Duncan shrugged.

"What kind of operation is this?" Thompson smiled. "They'll also need to be tested for gunshot residue."

"I got some sweats he can borrow," Duncan said.

"You can change in here while we question your mother down the hall," the trooper said.

"How do I know this isn't some scheme to get him alone," the mother said.

"Why are you so worried about him being alone?" the trooper said.

"I know the games you guys can play with a boy like him," she said. "I expect your mother would do the same for you."

"I expect you're right," the trooper said. "But I assure you we're not playing games. You have my word we won't question him without you."

"Then let's get it over with." She stood up from her chair.

"We have to wait a minute," Duncan said. "Mrs. Dennison's in the hall."

"I'd like to talk to her," the mother said.

"No you wouldn't," Duncan told her.

"How is Bobby?" she said.

"They're doing everything they can," the trooper told her.

"How is he?" she said. She looked to Duncan.

Duncan looked at the floor and shook his head.

"Please," she said. "Can't I talk to her?"

Duncan shook his head again. "I know you mean well, Donna, but you're about the last person I'd put in front of her right now."

At the car, Duncan opened the front door for the mother and the back for the boy. The sweatpants Duncan had given him didn't have a string, so he held a fistful of the waistband to keep them from falling. He cuffed the legs and he pushed the sleeves up over his elbows to keep them put. The boy slid onto the plastic seat in the rear of the car and pulled the door closed behind him. He felt the small tilt in the car as Duncan climbed in. The car shivered when the engine started.

"Now what?" the mother asked Duncan.

"Now we wait," he said. "The evidence, the tests got to come back."

The mother looked at him.

"So they can substantiate a story," he said. "Teddy claims Kevin loaded the gun but Kevin says the opposite. Unfortunately Bobby won't be around to say which is so. And neither me or Thompson is much in the mood to go bullying these kids at the moment. Not with what they seen today."

"But you said you knew it was an accident."

"We can't rightly say that," he said. "That was a mistake. Say Kevin is lying about loading the gun. Then we got to ask ourselves why he's not telling the truth. Did he get upset with his brother and whammo?"

"I don't think it was like that," the mother said.

"And even if it was an accident, that doesn't mean there won't be charges," he said. "Say it comes out that the gun was loaded before the boys even got there."

"No," she said. "Not a chance."

"I'm saying hypothetical, Donna. If that was the case they could bring charges of negligence on you and Pete, resulting in a loss of life. And if it was Teddy loaded it, he could get hit with the same—even reckless behavior. Same goes for Kevin."

"How could Teddy be guilty of anything if he wasn't even in the room?"

"If he left a loaded gun with two kids he knew had no experience with firearms?" Duncan said. "Some might see that as negligent or reckless behavior."

"This doesn't make any sense to me," she said.

"Well, so you know," Duncan said, "we got a mother with a dead boy who thinks that even owning a gun should be a crime."

She nodded. "How about that trooper—Thompson?"

"What about him?"

"Is he a good man?"

"I believe he is," Duncan told her.

"I know he isn't from here," she said. "But is he like us?"

"Donna? What does that mean?"

"You know exactly," she said. "Does he live in some condo and make his kids wear helmets when they walk down the sidewalk? Does he think it's a crime if a dog shits on the wrong lawn? Don't tell me you don't know what I mean, Dick."

"I think he's fine," Duncan said.

She nodded. "How long for the evidence?"

"Hard to say. This isn't the TV. The recession's hit the troopers hard. Thompson was telling me he had a murder case where he waited so long for a set of prints to come back that he finally sent them to his old precinct in Boston. And that was just one set of prints."

"How long?" she said.

"Couple months anyway," Duncan said. "Probably a safe bet."

They drove the rest of the way to the house in silence. In the driveway, Duncan stopped the mother before she could leave the car. "If either of you has any trouble, please call. We're always around and we know some good professionals."

"Excuse me?" the mother said.

"Counseling," he said.

"Oh, no." She batted a hand in the air. "That's okay."

"You know where to find us," he said.

"Thank you, but we'll be fine." She got out and opened the rear door for the boy, then headed up the walk, throwing a quick wave at Duncan as he backed out. She pulled open the spring-loaded screen door and the boy followed her inside. He kicked off his shoes, and climbed the stairs to the quiet privacy of his room. He sprawled on his bed and forced his face into the pillow, wishing he could crawl into some small corner of his room and hide. He wanted to slip behind the Sheetrock and stand there between the wall studs, waiting for everything to pass. He lay there for some time, breathing through his pillow, willing himself to disappear, wishing to be like Bobby— invisible and gone and blameless.

There was a soft knock at his door. He didn't respond, and it came again. The door opened and his mother softly called his name, but he didn't move. He tried to breathe as if he were sleeping. She called again and placed a hand on his leg, but still he didn't budge. After a moment, he heard the footsteps withdraw and the door close again.

When he lifted his head, there was a wet spot where his breath had soaked the cotton of the pillowcase. He sat up on the edge of his bed, his elbows on his knees and his head in his hands. He pushed on his eyes until it hurt. He pulled at handfuls of his hair.

"Stupid," he hissed. "Stupid. Stupid."

He drew his hand out away from his head and made a fist. He hesitated for a moment and then dashed himself with his knuckles. Each time he swung, there was less hesitation and the pop of his fist against his skull grew louder. When his knuckles grew sore, too sore, he started in with his other hand.

When it left him, after the feeling had burned out, he rested his head back in his hands and ran his fingers over the lumps on his scalp. He knew to do it above the hairline—he'd answered enough questions for the day.

Later in the night, after he heard his mother climb the stairs to her bedroom, after he gave her time to fall asleep, he made his way back down to the first floor of the house. Sleep seemed impossible. His mind raced with all of the things he could have done, and all the things that still might happen. His stomach ached and turned with hunger. He walked to the refrigerator and took out a plate of lasagna, covered in plastic wrap. He slowly pulled a drawer, eased a fork out, and headed for his room.

When he passed the dining room, he stopped. He left the plate and fork on the telephone stand in the corner and pushed the round button of the dimmer switch. He spun the knob to dull the glare of the small chandelier and walked to where Bobby had fallen. A rectangular patch of carpet was missing— cut out and taken as evidence by the troopers who had examined the room while they were at the station. The removed swath wasn't nearly as big as death would seem to demand.

The round had entered between two ribs, punctured Bobby's heart, and come to rest in his scapula. Since the bullet never left Bobby's body, there wasn't anywhere for the blood to go. It slowly pooled inside him.

The boy crouched and ran his hand over the carpet around the cutout. It didn't feel any different. He slowly dropped his nose—it smelled stale and a bit musty. He turned his face and looked under the cabinet, but the .22 was gone. He looked back to the vacant rectangle where Bobby had been and for a moment it struck him: Bobby Dennison was dead, and he would never be anything but that again.

4

Late that night, the father arrived from Pennsylvania. The boy heard the car pull in well after two in the morning and he quickly scrambled to kill his bedroom light. He stripped off his pants, threw them across the room, and crawled into bed. He heard the car door thump closed in the driveway and moments later he heard the front door of the house whine open. He heard the father's heavy footsteps in the house and then the dull, empty sounds of his parents greeting each other. As he listened, he practiced several poses of feigned sleep—on his back, mouth open, on his side, mouth slightly open, on his stomach, face concealed—but they never came for him. When they finally climbed the stairs, he heard them turn and head for their own bedroom.

The three ate a quiet breakfast together the following morning. The mother, still in her robe, cleared the kitchen table after the meal and left the room at the father's request. The boy and father sat kitty-corner to each other, the boy hunched, his head hanging. The father was barrel-chested and gray-haired. His elbows dug into the table, his eyes scrambled behind thick bifocals. As a child, the father had had a cyst removed from his left eyelid and now it sagged slightly. It gave him an inquisitive, untrusting look.

The father looked out from behind his brass-rimmed glasses and rubbed his graying stubble. A stiff, coarse sound came from between his hand and face. On weekends he sometimes waited until noon before making his pilgrimage to the bathroom where he showered and scraped the stubble from his heavy cheeks. He had trouble with the neck. The boy knew this from childhood, when he stood on the toilet seat and watched his father work the razor delicately around the peach pit of his Adam's apple.

Now the father sat at the head of the table, quiet, patient. This was the father's method: silence, silence for some time, and then a question, a question generally rhetorical in nature. It set the boy to floundering every time.

"So what are we going to do now?" the father said.

The boy shrugged.

"I know what you been through. With the law fixing to come down on you, I can't see throwing another log on the pyre."

The boy squirmed in his chair as a knot formed in his throat. This was another of the father's tactics: unexpected kindness. It worked to choke him up and send him reeling further.

The father shook his head and paused, perhaps to regain his composure. "I've heard what the police and your mother had to say. But I still can't figure how two kids got their hands on a gun in my house."

The boy looked down at the table.

"Well?" the father said.

"I showed them."

"Yeah?"

The boy shrugged. "They wanted to see it."

"So you do whatever any fool wants you to? You know what that makes you?"

The boy had trouble breathing. His throat started to close and his face grew tight.

"Who loaded that gun?"

The boy shrugged.

"Don't give me that."

"I don't know." The boy coughed it out.

"You realize that what you're saying makes no sense at all?"

"It must've been one of them," the boy said. "I didn't do it." He couldn't hold it back any longer and he went full-blown. His sniffling and gurgling were the only sounds in the room for some time. He used his shirt to wipe the tears and snot from his face.

"Quit the crybaby act," the father said. "It ain't going to work on me."

The boy didn't say anything.

"I hope you're not crying for yourself."

The boy shook his head.

"You best not be," the father said. "There's a dead kid out of this mess and a family who's got to live with that. Your mother's got to go teach in a school next week where every Tom, Dick, and Harry knows some kid just got himself killed in her dining room. And me, Ted, I'm a salesman. All I got is a reputation."

"I know," the boy nearly shouted. "Jesus, you think I ain't thought of all that?"

The father flinched. "Good," he said. "So this is what we're going to do. We're not going to say a word about it. Someone asks, you just shrug it off. Pretend like you don't know what they're talking about, like nothing ever happened. This rumor mill of a town doesn't need its fire stoked any more than it is. You get me?"

"Yes," the boy said.

"Good," said the father. "We're lucky we can leave. I don't know how we could stay here after something like this." He slid his chair back with a grunt. He stood and pushed the chair back under the table before he left the kitchen. Shortly after his departure, the mother returned from her seclusion in the living room. She rubbed the boy's back.

"You did good," she whispered.

"Ma. We can't do this."

"Yes we can."

"They're going to find out."

"It's your word against Kevin's," she said. "They can't prove anything."

He shook his head.

"If you don't play your cards right, they're going to take you away from me," she said. "And if that isn't enough, they've got something called a civil suit. They find us guilty of negligence or recklessness or God knows what else, those Dennisons will sue us and they'll win. You want to lose the house?" she asked him. "The cars? Everything?"

"No," he said and shook his head.

"Then you keep saying what you're saying. Understand?"

He didn't answer.

"Theodore," she said. "We can't take the gun out of Kevin's hands and we can't give that boy back to his poor mother. It's not going to happen. All we're doing is keeping you out of trouble. You get it?"

He nodded. His arms were folded on the table before him and he put his forehead in the crook of an elbow, hiding his face in the darkness his body created.

The father, son, and mother did what they could to duck one another's company for the next five days. They stuck to the father's policy—they didn't speak of the shooting, or Bobby's death, or what was to come. They came to the table for meals and they stared wide-eyed at the television in the evenings, but little was said among the three. The father busied himself with paperwork at a desk in the basement. The mother had two weeks' worth of the father's laundry to work through. The boy stayed in his bedroom and slept as much as he could. When he woke, he lay in bed, staring at the ceiling for as long as he could stand. He inventoried the contents of his bureau and closet, twice. He read random selections from a collection of encyclopedias he had on a bookshelf. Given the chance, his mind ground through the events around Bobby's death and his imagination ran off into the future, where he saw himself locked up in huge, clamoring institutions.

When he managed to get his mind away from the shooting, it took off with his fears of school. It started in the coming week. His small town was one of six that sent their students to a large regional high school—he was going from an eighth grade of ninety-five to a freshman class of over six hundred.

The day finally came when the father had to return to Pennsylvania and the house was busy preparing for his departure. The boy sat out of sight at the top of the stairs. He could see some of the interaction on the floor below in a mirror on the downstairs wall. His mother's brother, John, and his wife, Margaret, had come to see the father off. The father held the local paper that his brother-in-law had handed him.

"What?" the father said.

"Article on the editorial page," John said. "Look."

The father glanced quickly at the paper. "I don't have time for this." He handed the paper back.

"Ahem," John said, shaking the paper to attention. "'I think it is an outrage that a firearm was left accessible to young people.'" John paused and looked at the father. "This woman is trying to screw you."

"John," shouted the mother from another room.

"'I think it is time that gun owners are held responsible for any and all events that involve their firearms, even accidents.'" He let the paper down.

"I don't need this right now," the father said.

"She's trying to make it your fault," John said.

"John," the mother said, walking into the room. "Let it go."

"She has the right to say who can and can't go to the god-damn services," John said. "But this is too much."

"It doesn't concern you," she told him.

"How can you say that?" he said. "It's bullshit."

"Watch your language," the mother said. "I got a boy in the house."

The boy loved listening to his uncle cuss. He tried to swear with the same authority, but it always sounded cheap and phony.

"You think if you ignore it, it'll all go away," John said.

"One more word," she told him. "One more and you're gone."

"Donna," the father said. "Take it easy." There was a pause in the conversation. "John, we appreciate the concern, but I think it's just easier to let this lady do her thing. If and when they file charges, we'll do what we have to."

"This is your town," John said. "Both of you. You can't let her chase you out."

"Don't get dramatic on me, John—it doesn't suit you," the father said.

John didn't reply.

"There isn't work here," the father told him. "I can't live where there isn't work."

"It'll come back," John said. "Everyone's saying it."

"When it comes back, I'll come back."

"With women like this," John shook the newspaper. "There

won't be anything worth coming back to. It'll be one big sub-urb. Nothing but Volvos and Saabs."

"I guess the only thing left to do is get drunk and cry about it," the father said.

"Piss off," John said.

"Nice talk," said the father.

The boy heard the front door open and slam shut.

"Ted," the father hollered.

The boy waited a moment to give the impression that he'd been in his room. "Yeah?"

"Get down here."

The boy rumbled down the stairs.

"What?"

"Give me a hand." The father had a gun case in each hand. He pointed at two other cases on the floor. The boy took them up and followed him into the yard. The trunk of his Pontiac was open and half full, but the father went to Margaret's station wagon instead.

"What are you doing?"

"They're going to John's," his father said. "He's going to keep them for us."

"Why?" said the boy.

"You know why." The father took the two guns from him and slid them into the station wagon. "Come on," he said. They walked back into the house. The father made his way up the stairs to the boy's bedroom. He pulled a chair from the corner and sat down. He pointed at the bed and the boy sat, facing him.

"You all right?"

"Yes," the boy said.

"You're the man here now."

"I know."

"No more fooling around," his father said. "Time to batten down the hatches and pull it together, yeah?"

"Yeah," said the boy.

"You got to help your mother."

"I know."

"You ready for school?"

He shrugged.

"It ain't going to be easy."

"I know."

"Remember, just keep your head down, keep quiet, and let this thing blow over. I'll be back again in another week or two. If you have any trouble when I'm not here, you see John. You can't reach him, you call Dave Benson."

"Mr. Benson?" the boy said, surprised at the mention of an almost forgotten fishing partner of the father's.

"I know—it's been years. But he knows folks."

The boy played with the fringe at the edge of his bedspread. "How long you think?" he said. "Till the house sells?"

"It doesn't look good," the father said, "but you never know."

The boy nodded. He'd seen the real estate signs around town, the developments full of new, empty homes. He'd heard of people forced to sell their places for half of what they'd paid only a year prior. He'd heard worse. Notices of bank foreclosures and property auctions were showing up in the local paper with increasing frequency.

"You know, some places in Pennsylvania, kids get the first day of deer season off," the father said.

"Yeah?"

"Some schools even give the whole first week."

The boy smiled.

"Honest to God," said the father. "No kidding. It'll be just like the old days. Me and you, in the woods." He smiled at the boy and gave him a slap on the side of the shoulder with his heavy hand. The boy was afraid to speak. He thought his voice might crack and he would break into tears. He always felt overwhelmed when taken back into the father's good favor.

"Come on," the father said. "Let's get this show on the road. If I don't leave soon, I'll never get there."

In the driveway the father rearranged the contents of the trunk and slammed it shut. The mother and Margaret stood before the car and John appeared from the backyard and stood behind them. The boy sat on the front steps.

"No baloney now," the father said.

"Don't flatter yourself," John told him. The father smiled and the two men shook hands. Margaret stepped to the father next and kissed him on the cheek.

"Drive safe," she said.

"Always," said the father. He approached his wife and kissed her.

"Work hard," she said, softly rubbing his arm.

The father nodded, turned, and approached the boy. He reached out his hand and the boy shook it.

"Be good," the father said, clapping him hard on the shoulder.

The boy nodded.

"Two weeks," said the father. "Two weeks is nothing." He climbed into the driver's seat and slammed the door. The engine turned over and started and the transmission clunked into reverse. The father smiled and waved through the windshield before he looked over his shoulder and backed into the road. The horn blasted twice and they waved at the tail end of the Pontiac.

"Finally got rid of him," John said.

The boy smiled back but the women didn't.

"Don't worry about dinner," Margaret said to the mother. "I've got a shepherd's pie in the freezer."

The mother nodded. "Thank you," she said, and the two moved into an embrace. The boy watched as his mother pushed her face into Margaret's shoulder and Margaret slowly rubbed her back in circles. John skirted the two and approached him.

"Come on," he said. "Let's get out of here." John pointed at the passenger side of the station wagon and the boy walked to the side of the car. "You'll be over later?" John said to the women. They nodded and John got in the driver's seat. He started the car and drove the short distance to his house.

An oak bar stood in the back corner of the basement room. The head and antlers of two white-tailed deer hung from the back wall, next to a bearskin and a few mounted fish. Against the side walls stood well-crafted glass-faced gun cabinets, each lit from within, making them glow in the dull light. John had spent his tax refunds on the room, and while the rest of the basement lacked even Sheetrock, this room had hardwood molding. Margaret complained that the money could have paid for a vacation, and given the chance, John always replied, "That room *is* my vacation."

"You know where all these come from?" the boy said. He ran his finger around half the room, encompassing a good portion of John's gun collection in a single pass.

"I'd imagine," John said.

The boy walked over to a cabinet and opened it. "This one?" he said.

"A friend needed the money," John said. "Hit a kid in a crosswalk. Drunk."

The boy pointed at another.

"Estate auction."

He pointed again.

"Some fool didn't know what he had. I bought that for fifty bucks out of the want ads."

He stepped to the next cabinet down. "This one?"

"Me and your mother used to shoot that," John said. "We went to this dump as kids and went through the rubbish with sticks, for bottles and jars. We stood them on the side of an old icebox and I made up charges against them: disorderly conduct, drunk and disorderly, driving while drunk. We took turns until they were all shot up."

"Yeah?" said the boy.

"Don't tell her I told you, but we shot it at an oak door in the basement once. Had a bet whether or not it would go through."

"Who won?" said the boy. "The bet."

John shrugged. "It didn't go through. I know that. And deaf? My ears rang for a week."

The boy smiled and went on to the next cabinet. He opened the door and looked closely at an old pump-action shotgun.

"That was your great-grandfather's."

"I know. I never met him."

"Go ahead." He motioned for the boy to take up the firearm.

He hesitated.

"It's all right," John said. "It won't bite."

"That's okay." He tried to smile.

"Pick it up, Ted."

The boy reached into the cabinet and took it by the barrel. The action was open and he looked quickly to check the chamber.

"There you go," John said. "That's about as close as you're going to get to him. Without stepping in front of a bus anyway."

He pulled the stock to his shoulder. The wood was worn and smooth against his cheek. He let the gun down and looked it over again. It wouldn't have been the gem of anyone else's collection—the wood was nicked here and there and the blue steel had worn in places and shone silver. The boy used his shirttail to wipe it down before returning it. He looked at the next gun in the cabinet.

"Dad gave that to your mother for confirmation."

"What did you get?" the boy asked.

John shrugged. "I got that, when she got tired of it. She was his favorite."

"How come?"

"She went along with his stories," John said.

"What were his stories about?"

John squinted and looked at the ceiling as if to remember. "About how nice he was, how happy we all were. I tended to call his bluff."

"Why?"

"I couldn't help it," John said. "I guess I wasn't very good at telling stories."

The boy nodded as if he understood. He motioned to the next firearm in the row.

"Came back from World War Two with your great-uncle Dale's," John said.

The next cabinet down had just been stocked with the guns from the boy's home. He stood for a moment, staring through the glass.

"I know you've probably been asked this a hundred times," his uncle said. "But how you holding up through all this?"

"Fine."

"You sure?"

"Yeah."

"You want to tell me what happened?"

"Dad told me not to talk any more about it."

"Yeah, well, he's probably right."

"Besides," said the boy. "What's there to tell? Some kid killed his brother—you know that."

"I do," John said. "But that's a lot to carry. Whether you know it or not."

"You ever seen anyone die?"

John nodded. "Car accident," he said. "A woman got pitched from a truck when it flipped and it rolled right on over the top of her. She was terrible, head split open, arms and legs all twisted up. Gave me nightmares for weeks. Couldn't drive in the car for a while without getting these little spells where my heart raced and my breathing got all crazy."

"Bobby wasn't anything like that," said the boy. "You could hardly tell he was hurt. And I ain't had no nightmares."

"Well, just be careful," John said. "When it comes, it comes."

The boy nodded absentmindedly. His eyes were on the back wall. He walked over to one of the mounted deer. Its eyes were wide and glassy and the nose shone like it was still wet. He reached up and ran a hand down its thick neck, which felt stiff and hollow, the fur dry and brittle. He remembered the day his uncle had shot the buck. The boy had arrived just after John finished gutting it. The hind legs were splayed and steam rose from the empty carcass. Its eyes had already clouded over and the tongue that stuck out from between its clenched teeth was caked with dirt.

John cut the heart and the liver from the gut pile and he cut two feet of a branch with a wide fork at one end. He skewered the organs and slid them down until they came to rest on the Y where the branch split in two. He gave the stick a quick shake and when the makeshift handle proved suitable, he laid it to rest inside the deer and grabbed fistfuls of downed leaves to wipe the blood from his hands. Together, they noosed a rope around the animal's neck and front legs and dragged it back to John's house, where they hung it in a small shed. They went inside and John gave the boy his first beer. They said, "Cheers," and they drank.

5
———

The boy stepped down the three rubber-clad stairs and stood for a moment, looking out at the crowd, before he took the last step from the bus to the pavement. The driveway ran in a crescent in front of the school. Hordes of kids poured from their buses and crowds waited on the walk for friends to arrive. The red-brick bell tower stood high over them, the clock on its face off by hours. The boy saw a few people he recognized, but for the most part he stood surrounded by strangers.

He tried to stop and survey his surroundings, but the crowd behind him surged and forced him into the mob on the sidewalk. He bumped and squirmed through the maze of bodies and book bags. He saw Karen Hatch. She smiled, waved, and took quick little steps toward him.

"Hey, Teddy," she said. She leaned in and hugged him quick.

"Hey." He smiled. They weren't particularly close but he had known her since elementary school.

"There's so many new people," she said. "It's so exciting." He nodded.

She eyed everything around her except him.

"You seen Terry Duvall?"

She shook her head and he nodded.

"Well," she said. "See you."

"Yeah," he said.

"Good luck," she told him. She smiled and waved again before she walked away.

When he stumbled into some free space, he pulled a folded sheet of paper from his pocket. It was a map of the school he'd received in the mail several weeks back. The silhouette of each building was sketched on the paper with the names written inside. A star marked the location of his homeroom. He oriented himself, quickly stuffed the map back into his pocket, and set off for the star.

He rounded a corner and saw Darren Bell coming toward him. He smiled and tried to catch his eye, but Darren quickly looked at the pavement and passed without speaking.

The boy wondered how much they knew. He wondered if Karen's "good luck" was intended for the day of school or the investigation. He wondered if that was why Darren ignored

him. Since he was a minor, his name hadn't been released to the public, but that didn't mean much in their small town.

Two students sat in his homeroom when he arrived. He looked at the clock on the wall and saw that he still had another fifteen minutes before he had to be there. There was a 5-×-7 card on each desk. He found his name, sat, and pulled out his schedule and his map and plotted his course through the day. Then he rested his head on his folded arms and closed his eyes.

Before long the bell rang and students came pouring in. He recognized a few and nodded quickly at them. A huge kid with a shaved head took the seat behind him. He seemed older than the rest of the freshmen. After a few minutes he tapped a hard finger on the boy's shoulder. The boy turned. Without saying a word, the kid took hold of each side of his bottom lip and turned it out for the boy to see. On the inside of his lip, dark capital letters spelled out SKINS.

"It's killing me," he said once he had let his lip go. "Just got it done."

The boy nodded. Skinheads. He'd heard of them.

When the kid didn't say anything else, the boy turned around and put his head back on the desk. He tried to close his eyes, but they kept springing open.

He made his way to and from his first four classes without trouble, but a bottleneck in the hallway and the resulting crowd kept him from the lunchroom. The doorway had to accommodate both the inbound and the outbound traffic. He tried to edge his way into the single file that passed through the door, but no one would let him in. Just as a girl stopped and let the line move forward ahead of her, making room for him, he saw Kevin Dennison coming from the opposite direction. The boy froze and looked at the floor.

"You going?" said the girl who'd made room for him.

He shook his head.

"Fine," she snapped.

He turned and walked into the bathroom behind him. He went across the tile floor to one of the stalls and swung the flimsy door. It didn't quite fit in the frame, so he shouldered it shut. He sat on the toilet without pulling his pants down. The sounds of other students in the bathroom echoed around the walls of the stall.

Kevin Dennison had looked different. The boy couldn't place it exactly, but it was there. Maybe it was his face. His expression was stern, stoic. Perhaps it was the black T-shirt. Kevin was a prep in junior high and his outfits had included colorful collared tops and khakis.

The boy heard footsteps approach. Someone took the toilet next to him. He heard the flick of a lighter and soon he smelled smoke. He leaned forward and saw a familiar pair of work boots.

"Terry?" he said.

"Ted? The hell you doing in here?"

"Nothing," said the boy.

"You were pulling it, weren't you?"

He looked up and saw Terry, standing on the toilet, resting his elbows on the wall of the stall.

The boy shook his head. "You got an extra one of those?"

"An after-sex cigarette?"

"Come on." The boy waved his hand for one.

"What are you doing in here?" Terry reached down behind the wall and came up with his pack of Marlboros. He flicked the top open with his thumb and held it out to the boy. "You ain't taking a shit with your pants like that. Least I hope."

"Just taking a breather," the boy said.

"That's a good one," Terry said. "I'm going to steal that. Taking a breather." He inhaled hard on his cigarette and held the smoke in his lungs. "Take another one for later." Smoke poured out of his mouth as he spoke.

The boy stood and leaned against the wall opposite Terry. He put one cigarette behind his ear and held one between his lips.

"Suppose you need a light too." Terry reached down behind the wall again and his shoulder bobbed as he rummaged in his pocket. He leaned over the wall and lit the boy's cigarette. "Need one?" Terry held out the lighter to him. "I got another in my bag."

The boy nodded and took it. He focused on inhaling the way Terry had taught him. The smoke burned all the way down. He felt like coughing, but he held it back. The graffiti on the walls around him began to wobble and go crooked. He felt dizzy, so he sat back down. He liked the feeling. For a moment the two smoked in silence.

"So what happened?" Terry asked him.

"I can't talk about it."

"Come on."

The boy shook his head.

"That trooper came by my house," Terry said. "My parents loved that. I been meaning to say thanks."

The boy took another cautious drag.

"You told him we were on Darling's place."

"I had to."

"I sounded like a jackass, making some other story up," Terry said. "Then he told me you already told him."

"I had to say it."

"How long you figure until they know it was us setting the street on fire?"

"I don't think they care much about that."

"We'll see," Terry said. He stepped down from the toilet, out of the boy's sight. "I guess I should've known."

"What?" said the boy.

"You know. You can't ever keep your mouth shut."

"You don't know what you're talking about."

"Well," Terry said, "I know what I know."

The boy heard the quick hiss of Terry's cigarette hitting the water in the toilet. He heard the door of his stall whine open and bang shut.

"See you," he said.

"Yeah," Terry called back, the heels of his boots pounding the tile.

He stood and tossed what was left of his cigarette into the toilet. He flushed it with his foot and watched the butt circle and circle and eventually spin down the drain. He slid the second cigarette and the lighter into a small pocket of his book bag.

The crowd in the doorway to the lunchroom was gone when he got there. He saw Terry's orange hair above a table on the far side of the room. Terry sat with some older guys— the boy figured they were friends of Terry's brothers. He scanned the rest of the room and finally took a corner seat at a half-empty table. The nausea from the cigarette had stifled his appetite. He ate what he could of his lunch and then put his head on his folded arms and waited for the bell to ring.

His last class was in one of the portable buildings. They were long and narrow and looked like extended trailer homes. They sat between the tall bell tower and the four-story rectangle of the vocational building. In the late seventies the school had hauled the portables in as temporary classrooms for a sudden boom in the student body. More than a decade later they still housed history and social studies. He walked half the length of the hallway in the second portable to his American government class. The floor had a hollow, bouncy feel. When the door of the classroom closed, the whole wall seemed to shudder.

He knew his teacher from town. Mrs. Kimball had a son a year ahead of him and a daughter the year behind. She stood at the front of the class straightening papers on her desk. She put a folder in the drawer and called attendance. When his name came, he slowly raised his hand. He knew that every time he did so, he gave someone else the chance to put the name to his face, the chance to put his face in the stories they had heard.

Mrs. Kimball passed out her syllabus and gave an overview of what the class would entail. Students raised their hands and asked questions and she answered them. When the questions ceased, she began to outline their first assignment.

"Think about that old cliché assignment What I Did on My Summer Vacation," she said. "It's a little bit like that." She smiled and a few students laughed. "But I want it to be an analysis of something political that occurred over the summer. I want you to pursue your own interests. Doug, for instance, since he is interested in business, might want to focus on a specific interaction between government and the business world that occurred this summer. Some of you might be able to use some personal experience. Someone in this class might even be able to shed some light for us on the criminal-justice system." She looked directly at the boy when she said it, and he looked at his desk.

"Yes?" Mrs. Kimball said, acknowledging a hand somewhere behind him.

"Can I write about the gun debate?" a boy asked.

"In what way?" she asked him.

"Well, to start with, the ridiculous concept of blaming an inanimate object for our country's woes, and how that figures into the larger theme of liberal America's inability to accept responsibility for their own actions?"

Mrs. Kimball stood silently for a moment. "Do you have a specific event in mind?" she said.

"Of course," he said.

"What might that be?"

"I think you know what I'm talking about."

"I'm not a mind reader, Mr. . . . ?"

"Jackson," he said. "Jeffrey. Or J.J. But most people call me Peckerhead."

The class giggled. The boy tried to look over his shoulder but he couldn't get a glimpse of him.

"I don't think I'll be calling you that, Mr. Jackson."

"I'm just saying if you want to, I don't mind."

"I don't want this assignment to simply be a platform for your own political views, Mr. Jackson," Mrs. Kimball said. "It's an analysis of a specific event, with as much objectivity as possible."

"I'm sorry if I angered you," he said. "I meant no disrespect."

"You haven't angered me, Mr. Jackson."

"I come from a family where healthy debate is encouraged—that's all."

"I'm curious," Mrs. Kimball said. "Are your parents conservatives too?"

"I can only wish that was the case," Peckerhead said. "Bleeding hearts, the both of them."

The boy stood when the bell rang. He quickly packed his things and turned for the door. He looked at the ground. He feared that Mrs. Kimball would pull him aside and want to discuss what had happened with the Dennisons. He joined the herd at the doorway, waited his turn to leave, and hit a quick stride in the hallway. He didn't want to miss his bus.

"Theodore," someone called from behind him. It was the kid's voice from class.

He kept up his pace.

"Hey," the kid said. "Hey, man."

The boy looked when the kid grabbed his shoulder. Peckerhead Jackson was a skinny kid. Short brown hair, some acne. Black suspenders stood out from his white T-shirt. His khakis had long sharp creases.

"Don't call me that," the boy said. "It's Ted."

"Ted," he said. "Peckerhead." He held out his hand.

The boy shook it quickly. "Peckerhead?"

"Nobody forgets a name like Peckerhead." He smiled at the boy. "I didn't pick it."

The boy nodded.

"We had third-period bio together too. I sat three rows over."

"Yeah?"

"I was a little more reserved in bio. That was bullshit, what she pulled on you." Peckerhead pointed a thumb in the direction of the classroom that they had just left.

The boy kept walking.

"What are you doing after school?" Peckerhead said. "I got some friends. We all get together—you should come."

"So I can get a nickname like Peckerhead?"

"Funny. You're a ball-breaker—they'll like that."

"I got to run. I can't miss my bus." The boy quickened his pace, but Peckerhead kept up.

"We'll give you a ride. A few of the guys got cars."

"That's all right," the boy said.

"You like guns?" Peckerhead smiled. "We got a lot of guns."

The boy shook his head. He turned and jogged toward the drive where the buses idled.

"See you," Peckerhead called out.

The boy threw a hand up in a quick wave.

He had a dull evening of chores and homework and a quiet dinner with his mother. When he finished eating, he excused himself. He said he had homework and went to his room. He changed out of his school clothes, sat, and pulled a photo album out of his desk drawer. The leather cover was dry and cracked. The brown finish had worn off the edges and the corners were curled over. He liked to look at the pictures of his father in adolescence. He was pale, skinny, almost fragile-looking. On football teams where his father had insisted he was a standout, the boy saw that he was one of the smallest players. He always thought the realization should have been disheartening, but each time it actually let him breathe. The boy was a late bloomer. At fourteen, his armpits were bald and he still weighed less than most of the girls he wanted to date. The pictures made it easier. Sure he was skinny and hairless, but at least he was no worse than his father had been.

He turned the page to reveal four photos of several figures, heaped in winter clothes, standing on the vast, white expanse of a frozen lake. Their faces were so concealed by hoods and scarves that if it had not been for the father's stories, the boy would not have known who they were. The father and his father and brothers took to the ice when winter came, cut holes, and jigged for walleye and perch. But unlike the other fishermen—who drove trucks on the frozen lake and pulled shanties and sat around fires drinking schnapps—they stood some distance from one another and jigged away in silence. After they departed from the shore together, a toboggan loaded with gear in tow, the father's father would periodically auger a hole and leave a son, auger a hole and leave a son. They stood alone, weighed down in layer upon layer of wool, shifting from foot to foot, shivering. Rotating about the holes to keep their backs to the wind, they were sometimes envious of the houses on the shore, sometimes of the shanties, strewn like black pox on the ice.

When fish were caught, their skulls were dashed. Before they froze stiff, their bellies were slit and guts pulled free. The father spoke of reluctantly removing his mittens and with cold-blunted fingers opening the blade of his pocketknife. On good days, beside each hole grew a pile of fish and beside them grew a pile of their innards.

When the boy asked the father why they never heard from his brothers, the father told him that they weren't much different at home than they had been on the ice. Even in closer proximity, communication was functional and sparse at best. With the passing of their folks, there was little left to draw them together.

The boy clapped the album closed, put it away, and stood up from his desk. He opened the door and looked down the hallway. His mother was in her room, watching television. He closed the door, went to the window, and slowly eased it open. The screen proved a little difficult, but he got it off and out of the way. He rifled through his bag and came up with the cigarette and lighter. He killed the light in his room, stuffed pillows under his blankets and stepped out the window to the roof of the garage. The pitch was perfect to lie back on and look up at the sky. He thumbed the lighter, touched the flame to the cigarette, and drew in the smoke.

He inhaled slowly and methodically on the cigarette. He tried exhaling through his nose, but it burned much too badly. He thumbed the lighter again and stared into the flame. He started counting and got past fifty. His thumb began to burn and he stopped. He lifted his left arm and looked at his biceps. He pushed the searing hot metal into the soft pale flesh inside his arm. His whole body lurched and went tight at the feeling.

He closed his eyes and white light exploded on the backs of his lids. It took everything he had to keep it there. Once the burning went dull, he pulled the lighter back and slid it into the top of his sock. Without the burning he felt slow and heavy. The backs of his eyes went back to black. He let his head fall on the stone-dust shingles and he took a long slow breath.

6

___

Peckerhead Jackson approached the boy every day after school. He even sought the boy out before and after their third-period biology class. The boy tried to act uninterested, but it was difficult, since Peckerhead was the only person who tried to talk to him in the course of the school day. After a week of walking the halls alone, he started looking forward to Peckerhead's company. On the Tuesday after Labor Day weekend, Peckerhead approached him.

"You been thinking about us," Peckerhead said.

The boy shrugged.

"I'm not going to keep following you 'round like some whipped dog," he said.

"I never asked you to."

"Can't you see I'm trying to do you a favor?"

"I never asked for nothing from you."

"Would you quit being so stubborn and come on?"

"Yeah?" the boy said.

"Hell, yes," Peckerhead said. "Quit being so pigheaded." He smiled and the boy smiled back at him. He followed Peckerhead out to the school parking lot, where a group of guys stood in a circle. Many of them had on the same outfit as Peckerhead: black suspenders, white T-shirts, pressed khakis. The group parted as Peckerhead and the boy approached. A handful of the closest boys stood staring.

"Guys, this is Ted LeClare. He's a freshman."

Most of the group smiled and a handful called out a greeting to him. The two closest to him held out a hand and he shook them. An older guy hopped off the trunk of a car and walked toward him. The crowd parted.

"Theodore LeClare, nice to finally meet you," he said. "I'm George Haney."

"Ted," the boy said. He reached out to shake George's hand. "Just Ted."

George smiled and they shook. The boy noticed that his hand was small for his age, his handshake a bit weak. George was also somewhat pear-shaped. He had narrow shoulders and wider hips. "How is school treating you?" George asked.

"Fine."

"Anyone giving you trouble?"

The boy shook his head. There was something to the way George spoke. He looked the boy in the eye and patiently waited at the end of each question. The boy felt as though his answer mattered.

"He likes guns," Peckerhead called out from the other side of the group. "I told him you'd show him."

"I didn't say that," the boy said.

"You don't have to be ashamed." George said it slowly and shook his head. His demeanor was calming to the boy. "We're all red-blooded Americans here. We like guns too." He smiled.

The boy smiled back.

"I have to work for a couple hours at my mother's shop," George said. "There won't be many customers. If you'd like to come along, we can chat and I can give you a ride home when I get off."

The boy shrugged.

"You'll be home for dinner," George said. "Come on." He was easy to listen to and the boy followed him through the crowd to his Ford sedan.

The store was small, just an addition off their single-story ranch house. The sign out front read VIRA'S PANTRY. GUNS, AMMO, KNIVES, HUNTING ACCES., HOME PROTECTION. He followed George across the dirt parking lot. It was uneven and rutted out. An electric chime rang as George opened the front door. His mother sat behind the register reading a magazine. Behind her stood a vertical row of at least thirty rifles and shotguns. Above them on the wall hung what looked to be an M16, an AK-47, and two other assault rifles the boy didn't recognize. In front of her was a long glass display case full of handguns and knives. When they got close, she looked down at her watch and shook her head. She was a big woman with

short gray hair, but when she shook her head, the boy saw that
it was long in the back.

"Would it kill you to get here on time?" she said.

"I have school, Mother," George said.

"Don't give me that."

"You can go now," he told her.

"I know what I can and can't do," she said. "Don't get
lippy just 'cause one of your little peckerwood friends is here."

"I'm sorry, Mother."

"I told you not to give me that tone."

"Fine," he said. "Just leave."

The boy was startled by the jump in George's voice. He had
walked down one of the aisles, toward the back of the store,
to get away from the argument.

George's mother shook her head. The floor creaked as she
walked across the room and he heard the door that led into
their house open and shut.

"I apologize for that," George said.

"It's nothing."

"I find it very embarrassing."

"Don't," said the boy.

"She doesn't agree with my attempts to better myself. She
says it's bad for business, if you can believe that," George said.
"It kills her that we're going under. I'm sure you've noticed
our lack of inventory."

The boy had noted the sparsely stocked shelves, but he
shrugged as if he didn't.

"You're kind, but the truth is that we've lost our credit
with most of our suppliers."

"My dad had to move to find work," the boy said. He

walked over to the glass case and peered in at the selection of handguns. George went behind the counter and stood across from him. The boy was fascinated by the revolvers. He loved the exposure of their firing mechanisms. The newer semiautos tucked away most of their moving parts, but with the revolvers, it was all there to be seen.

George unlocked the case and reached inside. "Hold this one," he said. George pushed a pistol into the boy's hand. "That's German design, German manufacture."

"It's heavy," the boy said.

"That's partly the age of the piece, the lack of materials technology that we have today, but it's also due to the exceptional caliber of the round." George set a large bullet on the glass counter. "That, Ted, would do considerable—" He was interrupted by the electronic chime of the front door. Another teenager stepped into the shop. The first thing the boy noticed was his shaved head.

"What's up," the other boy said, throwing a casual, salute-like greeting at George.

"Jason," George said. "I was just showing this young man the Luger."

"He's a tease," Jason said to the boy. "He ain't let me shoot it yet."

"You can shoot it when you buy it," George told him.

"And just give me a minute to sell my car and whore-out my mother," Jason said. He laughed with George. The boy smiled.

"Jason Becker, Ted," George said.

Jason Becker reached out to shake his hand.

"Good to meet you, Ted," said Jason. "Sorry I can't hang—my mother's got me by the short ones. Tonight?"

"Of course," George told him.

"I'll be there," Jason said. "See you around."

"Sure," the boy said. After the door closed he asked George if Jason was a skinhead.

"No," said George. "He's Youth."

The boy shrugged.

"American Youth," George said. "It's a small group I coordinate. We get together and discuss politics, activism, that kind of thing. You should come."

"Maybe," the boy said.

"Definitely," George told him. "Tonight—think you can?"

"I can call my mom and ask."

"Good," George said. "The phone's back here behind the counter."

The boy was nervous. He sat in the center of a circular booth, surrounded on all sides by George's cohorts. They held meetings at the local Denny's, a twenty-four-hour chain diner. On his right sat Jason Becker, the largest and most intimidating of the bunch. If George was the leader, Jason seemed a second-in-command of sorts. He was the brawn to George's brains. To the right of Becker sat Peckerhead, who kept opening his mouth to speak but never said much more than a few words before he was interrupted. On the boy's left sat Dan; when George introduced him he made it clear that Dan was captain of the varsity wrestling team. Beyond Dan sat Birch, a tall, lanky guy with an enormous pompadour. George pulled a chair up to the open spot at the table and sat. Behind him a group of young cadets moved their chairs and crooked their necks to try to get closer to the action in the booth.

"What do you think?" Jason Becker asked the boy.

The boy shrugged.

"You know it's their welfare spending killing the economy, keeping your dad out of work," Becker said.

"My dad has a job," the boy said.

"Simply put, Ted, I'm an American," George interrupted from across the table. "I believe in freedom." He took a breath. "I personally don't think that people in New Hampshire should have to live like people in Rhode Island or Alabama. Or them like us, for that matter. I believe in America the republic, where the power is equally dispersed among the states." Taking a sip of coffee, George shushed someone else at the table with an open palm raised in the air. "But if you're a Federalist—they call themselves Democrats but they have nothing to do with democracy—if you're a Federalist, Ted, you think that the national government has the right to force the same laws over everybody, with no concern for local culture or community."

"Dude, it goes way back," Peckerhead said. "Alexander Hamilton and Thomas Jefferson were having the same argument."

"Civil War," Becker said, holding up a finger to make a point. "All that slave stuff was secondary to the real conflict. The North wanted to force a trade tariff on all the states. The South wanted the right to make laws on a state-by-state basis."

"These days all they preach is diversity, but it's just the new hegemony," George said. "If they're going to embrace the Hollywood whores and homosexuals, they also have to accept those of us who don't greet them with open arms." George's voice rose in energy. "They can have the whole of California, for all I care. Massachusetts, Connecticut—keep them." He paused and raised an index finger in the air above the table. "Just as long as we can keep what's ours." George brought a fist down on the table, rattling the plates and silverware there.

"Hell, yeah," Becker said. He reached up and gave George a high-five.

"I'm not here to tell anyone else how to go about their business," George said. "But I'll be damned if anyone comes into my home and tries to tell me how I got to live."

High-fives went around the table. They smiled and punched fists. The boy found himself consumed by the energy in the booth. Goose bumps grew on his forearms and when Dan held up his hand, the boy reached up and slapped it hard. Becker threw a jab at the boy's shoulder and slapped him hard on the back. The boy didn't understand it entirely—George had lost him somewhere around *hegemony*—but whatever it was, it felt good.

The Youth wardrobe was influenced by both the professional golf tour and the local skinheads. Loafers and argyle socks were a mainstay and their khakis were hiked up to show them off. Narrow black suspenders stood out against their white T-shirts.

Much of the community adored the Youth. In school they

acted as a sort of underground vigilante force. They ratted out drug dealers and finked on folks who boozed before the pep rallies. They went to church and took part in volunteer organizations to support their view that social welfare was the obligation of the community and not the federal government. They organized protests against anything that defied what they thought to be good, wholesome, and true. They organized protests against protests.

After they left Denny's, it was clear the Youth members had another destination in mind, but they made a detour and dropped the boy off at home before he could discover where they were headed.

"Think about it, Ted," George said.

The boy nodded. He stood in his driveway, outside George's car window.

"You're with us, man, I know you are," George told him. "But you have to make up your mind."

The boy nodded again.

"Have a good night, Ted," George said. There were other farewells from within the car.

"See you," the boy said. The car backed out and they were off.

The boy stood for a moment facing the empty road. He turned and looked at his house. His mother was home, but the only evidence of her presence was the flickering light of the television in the living room. He walked to the mouth of the driveway and looked again at the house. When he didn't see her, he walked across the yard and took hold of the real estate sign. He wrenched it out of the ground and jogged across the street.

He took the sign by the legs, spun several times, and let it fly. It wobbled in the air like an unbalanced Frisbee, clanged into a good-size pine, and crashed into the underbrush. He loped back across the street and down his driveway.

Inside the house, he kicked off his shoes and walked into the living room. His mother sat on the couch with an afghan over her legs.

"Where you been?" she said.

"I told you," he said. "Out."

She looked at him.

"Denny's, with those guys, the ones I told you about."

"Tell me again."

"They're a group. Like an organization."

"They got a name?"

"American Youth," he said. "They're political."

"Political?" she said. "What the heck's a kid your age got to be political about?"

"Plenty, Ma. They're against drugs and alcohol. They're for American values."

"That's political, huh?"

"Why wouldn't it be?"

"Just seems strange for teenage boys to get excited about something like that."

"That's why it's political, Ma."

"Take it easy," she told him. "If it's going to keep you out of drugs and liquor, go ahead and be political then."

"They don't like the new people in the developments either."

"Why not?"

"Because they're trying to change everything here."

She nodded. "Not troublemakers or anything?"

He shook his head.

"You can't get in trouble," she said.

"I know."

"I'm not kidding, Theodore. You get in trouble again and it could ruin everything. You hear me?"

He nodded. "You heard anything?"

She shook her head. "Dick Duncan said if I called anymore he'd file harassment charges. You?" she said. "Anything going around school?"

"I'm sure they talk," he said. "They don't say it to me, though."

She nodded. Her eyes stayed on the television. "I left dinner on the stove."

He turned to walk into the kitchen.

"Hey," she called.

He stopped and turned.

"Would you quit throwing that sign?"

He looked at her.

"I'm not getting it this time." She still looked at the television.

"It doesn't matter whether it's there or not," he said. "People don't buy houses where that happened." He pointed in the direction of the dining room.

"Stop that," she told him. "Stop it now."

"Why?" he said. "It's the truth."

"Does it make you feel any better to think that the house will never sell and we'll be away from your father for good?"

He shook his head.

"So why think that way?" she asked him. "The truth doesn't matter."

He nodded and looked at the television. He turned and walked into the kitchen, stopping for a moment at the entrance of the dining room to look in. It was dark and he could just make out the outlines of the table and chairs, the china cabinet. His mother had thrown a decorative rug over the missing rectangle of carpet, but it was hard for him not to think about it. It was hard not to think about how different everything could be.

1

Following another day of school, an afternoon at the Haneys' shop, and an evening spent at Denny's, the boy loaded up with the Youth and headed out again. He sat with two others in the back of George's Ford sedan. Peckerhead was in the front, next to George. Four other guys were packed into Jason Becker's Volkswagen Rabbit—the car was covered with such a skin of stickers and graffiti that at first glance it looked like something from the circus. But a closer look at the slogans made it clear that a crowd of clowns wasn't about to pile out: BURN MY FLAG AND I'LL BURN YOUR ASS; KILL A COMMIE FOR MOMMY; ABORTION = HOMICIDE; A FIRESTORM TO PURIFY.

George turned off the bypass and plunged into darkness, leaving the lights of the strip malls and gas stations behind them. It was a rainy night and the wipers cut back and forth across the windshield. The boy was excited to see that they weren't heading in the direction of his home. He wondered where they were off to. It surprised him when he looked over his shoulder and saw that Becker's Rabbit no longer followed them. George pushed a tape into the car stereo and some loud music spilled from the speakers. The boy tried to listen to the lyrics but the singer was indecipherable. Peckerhead pounded his fists on the dashboard of the car to the beat of the music.

George pulled into one of the new housing developments and the boys glared out the windows of the car.

"Here, here, here," Peckerhead said. "Stop!" he shouted. He pushed open the door of the car, jumped to the pavement, and ran toward the mouth of a driveway. Through the rain-speckled rear window of the car, the boy watched him squat and get hold of a good-size ceramic flowerpot. He raised it over his head and dashed it to the pavement. The two adjacent flowerpots suffered a similar fate. The boys in the backseat of the car cheered him on. George had killed the headlights and he scanned their surroundings for any potential witnesses. Finished with the flowerpots, Peckerhead got both hands on a small cedar and ripped it from the ground. He shook it victoriously over his head and tossed it to the far side of the street. Then he attempted to tear down the mailbox. When it wouldn't budge, he ran back to the car.

"Go! Come on, go!" he yelled as he jumped into the front seat. He was wet from being out in the rain and his breathing was heavy. The boy looked back again to see the broken pottery, the black soil spilled out over the flowers. The tree lay limp and alone where it had been thrown. It could probably be replanted, the boy thought.

"It's like this," George said after he'd turned the headlights back on and accelerated to a suitable speed. "Vandalism is a form of protest."

"Hell, yeah," Peckerhead said. "The German tribe shit, tell him the German tribe shit . . ."

"Peckerhead," George said, holding up an index finger. "I'm getting there." George turned onto another road of the development. "The Vandals tore up the Roman temples to protest the encroachment into their territory." George looked to see if he was satisfied and Peckerhead nodded. "These people are encroaching on us."

"They don't belong here," Peckerhead said.

George navigated the car through the maze of the development and the boy could tell that they were on the lookout for another display to assault.

"How do you know?" the boy said.

"What?" George said.

"How do you know?" the boy said again.

"How do we know what?" George said.

"That they're Federalists."

"Look," George said. "Do these houses look like our houses?"

The boy looked at George's reflection in the rearview mirror.

"Damn," Peckerhead suddenly burst out. "This is my favorite shirt." George hit the interior light and Peckerhead held the fabric up to show everyone that the rain had caused his black suspenders to bleed onto his white T-shirt. Earlier in the night the boy had noticed that the shirt had a simple depiction of Reagan's face on the front. The two other boys in the backseat now lifted their own suspenders to see if their shirts had suffered a similar fate. They'd been spared but the boy could tell that Peckerhead's experience had seriously stifled anyone's interest in further action. There were no more requests for George to stop, even though the boy saw several appealing targets: a mailbox in the shape of a swordfish, a water fountain that glowed the color of a healthy pumpkin, a false well house with bucket, rope, and hand crank.

A large illuminated sign stood at one of the exits of the development. It was wooden, the letters ornately carved and painted: WESTCHESTER ESTATES. The car stood at the intersection as the boys bent their necks down to see it atop a small knoll. Cars passed more frequently on the road the development spilled out onto.

"Westchester, my ass," Peckerhead hissed. He kicked open the door and jumped out of the car.

"Peckerhead," George yelled. He rolled down his window. "Peckerhead," he said again. "The goddamn road."

Undaunted, Peckerhead marched up the hill to the sign. George panicked a little and finally backed the car up, away from the main road, with the door still open. The boy reached forward and closed it, turning out the interior light. It was quiet in the car as they watched Peckerhead do everything he could to try to bring the sign down. He karate-kicked it twice, then got a running start and threw his shoulder into it. The sign held its ground and Peckerhead stumbled backward, rubbing his arm. He ran at it again and clambered awkwardly atop the sign. He shifted his weight back and forth in an attempt to loosen it from its footing. The sign didn't budge and Peckerhead eventually lost his balance and fell to the ground. The boys in the car flinched at his landing. Peckerhead scrambled back to his feet, picked up a rock, and smashed the lights that illuminated the wooden facade. When he got back to the road, he turned and hurled the rock at the sign, missing it by a foot or so.

George drove the car out onto the bypass and eased it up to the fifty-five-mile-per-hour speed limit. In response to the general feeling of defeat that lingered in the car, George began a lecture on the new local economy: "They want their Egg McMuffins and coffee on their commute—"

"What the hell is that?" Peckerhead cut in. He looked at George and then the boys in the backseat. He held out his hand and it shook in the air. George looked around the dashboard for some sort of sign. The shimmy quickly progressed, and soon the entire car shuddered.

"Pull over," the boy said, but George kept driving. The thumping began, getting louder, quickly louder, and the car shook more violently.

"I messed up my car," George said with a sad confusion in his voice.

"Pull over," the boy said again, and George finally let it coast into the breakdown lane.

Outside they stood in a semicircle, staring at the smoking rear tire. There was an awe among them, an awkward silence that confused the boy. They were frozen.

"We're sitting ducks," Peckerhead said.

"The cops can't prove anything," George told him.

"I'm more worried about the guy whose place I just tore up," Peckerhead said. "Getting vigilante on us." He rubbed the top of his head and looked back and forth in either direction on the dark road.

It suddenly became clear to the boy what the problem was: These guys didn't know how to change a tire. "Pop the trunk," he said.

Even though he didn't destroy a single Federalist lawn ornament, the boy still ended up the hero of the night. There were pats on his back and high-fives, and when they met up with the others back at Denny's, they all began calling him Teddy the Mechanic. By the end of the night it had been shortened to Teddy the Wrench, and the boy liked this very much.

He liked it all very much. He liked the handshakes, the smiles, the older guys telling him he'd do just fine with them. He started to see that everything that was good in the world was a result of honest American values. Anything bad was a result of a departure from those core principles.

Those kids in seventh grade, the ones that made fun of him because his sneakers only *looked* like Nikes: fucking Federalist assholes.

George didn't want to drive far on the spare tire, so Jason agreed to take the boy home. Some angry music spilled from the tape deck and the two spoke little. The boy was surprised when the car slowed and Becker turned into the Sandy Creek development. For a moment he thought Becker had taken a wrong turn. He was about to say something when Becker looked over and said, "This is for you, Teddy." He throttled the car. "Hold on," he said.

The car quickly accelerated and the boy reached up and grabbed the handle above the door. With his left hand he reached down and got a good grip on the bottom of the seat. The Volkswagen barreled onto the fresh-cut lawn, mowed with the precision of a fresh flattop. Becker spun the wheel sharp and wrenched up on the emergency brake. The car went into a wild power slide and the tail end came almost all the way around. When the car came to a rest, Becker threw it into reverse, floored it, and cut the wheel. As they spun, the boy saw the lights of the house come and go, come and go from his field of vision. The car was filled with the noise of the racing engine and the clatter of soil and stone pummeling the wheel wells. They came to a stop and the boy heard the music again. Becker shifted and drove quickly back to the road. He looked over to the boy.

"We haven't forgotten," he said.

"What?"

"That they tried to blame you for what happened."

"How do you know where they live?"

"Mrs. Dennison?" Becker chuckled. "Man, she's high on our list. We've been sending her anonymous hate mail since she made her debut on the town council."

"Why?" the boy said.

"Don't give me that naïve crap," Becker said. "This isn't some little game. This is our town. This is everything."

The boy sat on the edge of the bed with his head in his hands. He didn't feel good about the Dennisons' lawn. He didn't feel good about the hate mail. He still didn't feel good about Bobby, not even okay. He saw Kevin around school and he could see that he didn't feel so good about it either. Kevin wore high combat boots and his hair was shorn unevenly. He wore a lot of black. He had the look of a boy with troubles.

The boy ran the fingers of his right hand under the sleeve of his T-shirt, along the inside of his left arm. A fingernail caught on the edge of scab and he picked at it. The most recent burn was swollen and tender to the touch—his fingers jumped away from the blistered flesh. Each time, he swore it was the last. For a spell of days and nights he could keep away from it, but when his mind got to racing, he always justified another.

He couldn't say why he did it, or why it felt so good. He just knew that when he did it, he became the burning, he became the pain, and when he was the pain, he didn't have to be anything else.

8

After school the next day, a small entourage of Youth members took the boy on a trip to the mall. After leaving one of the larger department stores, Becker motioned for the others to follow him. Once in the bathroom, Becker pulled a pair of black suspenders out of his pants. He saw the look of surprise on the boy and said, "Corporate chains rob us blind." The boy put on the suspenders. Before they left the bathroom, Becker said, "Cuff up your pants." In doing so the boy further exposed the old pair of loafers Becker had traded him for a Wrist-Rocket slingshot. Birch leaned back and kicked open the bathroom door. It resounded with a boom and the boom's echo, but the boy never flinched. The four of them hit their stride on the concourse. The boy's skin rose in goose bumps and static tingled in his scalp.

After the mall, Jason and the boy went to the gun shop to wait for George to get off. They sat around reading the magazines that collected in the shop. George's girlfriend walked through the door, setting off the electronic chime. The boy looked up from the most recent copy of *Soldier of Fortune*. He thought she was cute—Colleen Crenshaw—with her sad eyes and the nose ring that George hated. Colleen and George smiled and kissed over the counter.

"Mom's going to let me off early," George said.

"What do you want to do?" She bent over and rested her head in her hands. Her elbows sat atop the glass gun case. She wore a short skirt and the boy tried desperately not to stare. They were both in ninth grade, but Colleen was a year and a half older than he was. She had a driver's license and a blue Ford Escort.

George shrugged. "You?" he said.

"Let's go shopping."

"Yeah?"

She nodded.

When George's mother arrived, the four climbed into Becker's car. George insisted on riding in the front seat, leaving Colleen and the boy cramped together in the back. Colleen leaned in to speak to him, so close as to send soft washes of breath against his ear. This perpetuated flurries of what felt like electricity to the ends of his limbs. When the car turned, she reached down and took hold of the boy's thigh to steady herself. When they stopped to stroll through music shops and pawn shops and used-clothing stores, the boy couldn't wait to return to the cramped backseat of the Volkswagen.

They stopped at a barn that had been converted into a large indoor flea market. On summer weekends, stands and tables covered much of the old pasture, but during the week they vanished and the market retreated inside the musty barn. Jason said it was a great place to find switchblades and billy clubs. The barn was mostly filled with old odds and ends of furniture, but there were the occasional glass cases that held strange collections of coins, knives, thimbles, and sports cards. George and Colleen had taken off on their own as soon as they arrived, leaving Becker and the boy to stroll by themselves.

"I always wanted one of those," Becker said.

The boy stood at his side. "The racetrack?"

"Box looks brand new," Jason said.

The boy nodded.

"Ten bucks," Jason said as he fingered the stringed price tag. "Way too much." He walked around a corner. "Hey," he called out. "Come here a minute."

An old man scuffled over in a pair of slippers. He looked at Jason.

"What's the best you can do on this?" Jason said.

"What's it say?"

"Ten bucks."

"Well," the old man said. "You can read."

"Ten?" said Jason. "Come on. I got five." He held out a wad of bills.

"Get another five off your buddy and you got a deal." The old man smiled.

"Probably doesn't even work," Jason said.

"I took a couple laps on her myself. Just to be sure."

"I need a birthday present for my little brother," Jason said.

"Seven," the old man told him.

"Six," Jason said.

"Six?"

"Six," said Jason.

The old man finally nodded and the two carried out the transaction. The old man smiled, said thanks, and shuffled back to his post. Jason took up the package. "I'll take this out to the car," he told the boy. "You go and get them two."

The boy nodded and proceeded to wander about the barn. When he didn't find them on the first floor, he headed up into the loft. He was about halfway up the stairs when his head cleared the second floor. In a gap between two pieces of furniture, he caught sight of George and Colleen. He had moved past the opening and he had to lean back to see them again. Colleen sat high on a bureau and George stood between her legs. Her arms were wrapped around his neck and their heads moved back and forth as they kissed. The boy's breathing quickened. He knew he should call out or head to the car and wait, but he didn't move. Colleen took an arm from around George's neck and reached down to take hold of his wrist. She pulled his hand up to her breast and moved it in slow circles. George suddenly pulled his hand away and let it fall back to its place on the bureau. She tried to take hold of his wrist again but George held firm and then withdrew from their embrace.

"How many times have I told you?" he said.

She smiled at him.

"It's not funny," he said in a harsh whisper.

"I don't think feeling me up is going to get you sent to hell."

"One thing leads to another. Then what?"

"I don't know," she said slowly. "Then what?"

"Stop it," he told her.

She pulled him close and began whispering in his ear. George pushed her arms off of him and quickly stepped back. "Goddammit," he said. "Why do you have to be such a slut?" He turned and walked away from her. When he rounded the corner to the stairwell, he came face-to-face with the boy. Neither spoke, they stared, wide-eyed, at each other.

"I was just coming for you," the boy said finally. "Jason sent me. He's out at the car."

George rumbled past him on the stairs. "Let's get out of here," he said. Colleen came around the corner of the stairs and caught the boy's eye. He looked up and she wowed her eyes at him. She mouthed the word *Oops* and put a hand on his shoulder as she passed him.

In the backseat of the car the boy slouched under the box of the electric racetrack. It protruded from the hatchback, just over his head, and cramped him further in the already small space.

"You're going to get a crick in your neck," Colleen said. She smiled. She reached up and massaged his shoulder, working her small fingers up to his neck and then to the back of his head. He held his breath. He looked up to the front of the car. Jason and George were having a loud conversation over the

loud music from the stereo. "Don't worry," she told him, her
hand still working on him. "They're busy."

He quickly looked away from her, out the window.

That evening, Jason Becker's mother went out on a date and a
significant portion of the Youth congregated at his apartment.
The boys crowded around the television in the living room,
where they watched a videotape of a band whose political
platform cohered with their own. The bald, bare-chested
singer screamed out precisely what was wrong with the world.
Heads rocked to the steely and static-ridden music that
squawked from the television speaker. There were shots of the
sweaty and seething crowd—fists shot into the air and the
mob surged here and there as a whole, like a collection of
small fish or birds.

"All right, all right," the singer said between songs. "Take
care of each other out there. You might've heard this next
one . . . 'Take It Back.'"

George and Colleen sat at the back of the crowd, in the
kitchen, the boy across the table from them. The racetrack
wound in a figure eight on the floor and electric cars sped
around under the command of two triggered controls in Jason
Becker's hands.

"He's so cute," Colleen said quietly. She pointed at Jason.

The boy looked and smiled.

"Want to go for a walk?" she asked George.

George shook his head. His eyes were on the television
across the room.

"I knew you wouldn't," she said. "Teddy?" She looked at
him.

He shook his head.

"Come on," she said, standing. "Take me for a walk." She came around the table and took his hand.

He looked at George.

George made a motion with his head and the boy got up. He felt awkward walking through the crowd with his hand in Colleen's, so he pulled it free. He followed her outside and around the corner of the apartment complex. She rifled through her purse and came out with a cigarette and a lighter.

"What are you doing?" he said, louder than he had expected to.

"Want one?" she said.

"You're going to get me killed."

"I have gum."

He stayed silent for a moment, looking at her. Colleen's face didn't change.

"No thanks," he said. He walked in small circles while she smoked. He could see the lights of their high school in the distance, but he didn't want to think about school. Without his father around, he had little energy for his studies. He knew his grades were lagging already this quarter and he knew he would hear about it from his father, but he also knew he wouldn't have to hear about it for long. His father would be home to bark at him for two or three days and then be gone again for two or three weeks.

"What was it like?" Colleen suddenly said. She took a drag off her cigarette and exhaled. "When that boy died?"

The boy balked and for a moment he was speechless. "I'm not supposed to talk about it," he finally said.

"How come?" she said.

"There's an investigation."

"Could you go to jail?"

He shrugged. "I don't know," he told her. "How do you know about it?"

She chuckled. "Everyone knows about it, Ted. Why do you think they're so interested in you? You're like their cause."

The boy stared out into the darkness. He was about to ask for a cigarette when Youth members began streaming out the door behind them. Colleen dropped her cigarette, stepped on it, and exhaled before turning around. George approached them.

"You need to go home," he told Colleen. "Come on, Ted."

"What?" she said. "No way."

"You smell that, Teddy?" George said. "That smell like cigarettes to you?"

"Fine," she said. She walked over and hastily kissed him on the cheek.

"Good night," George told her.

At the parking lot, the Youth divided among several cars. The boy found himself in George's mother's sedan.

"I don't think it's cool," Peckerhead said.

"This is not about thinking," George replied. "This is principles."

"His parents," Peckerhead said. "They just divorced, for crap sake."

George didn't respond.

"I'm not doing this," Peckerhead said. "Screw this."

"You don't have to," George said. "I just wish you wouldn't make up excuses."

"What does that mean?" Peckerhead said.

"You don't have the stomach for this kind of thing," George said. "Fine, but don't make excuses for Dan when they're really for you."

"Fuck you," Peckerhead said.

"Fuck me?" George said. He paused for a moment. "I expect better from you, J.J."

No one spoke for the rest of the ride. They stopped behind a supermarket not far from their high school. No one else was there. They got out and the boy was glad when George pulled him aside and whispered, "Stay back—let the veterans take care of this."

Becker's car arrived shortly. He and Birch climbed out of the front seat and several of the younger guys weaseled out from the backseat. Another car rolled in with another couple of guys. The group mingled about until they had effectively isolated Dan.

In a very formal tone, George said, "You've been untrue to us, Daniel." He paused. "You were drinking at a jock party last weekend."

"No way," Dan said.

"Are you calling me a liar?"

"Not you," Dan said. "Whoever said it."

"I'm saying it," George said.

Dan didn't reply.

"If you come clean, we can begin to forgive you," George said. "But this, this gets us nowhere."

"Fuck this," Dan said.

There was a moment of silence.

George walked back to the crowd.

Two of the younger guys stepped forward and tried to get

ahold of Dan's arms, but he shucked them both. They tried again, and again he shucked them, shoving one in the chest and one with a palm to the face. The two stepped back and Becker moved in. Becker swung and Dan ducked, lurched forward, and got ahold of Becker's upper body. He heaved Becker off the ground and toppled him to the pavement. With Becker lying on his back, Dan could've easily kicked him, but he didn't—he kept moving, not allowing the group to corner him against the building.

Birch stormed in and dived at Dan's hips, but Dan sprawled his legs back and forced Birch's face to the pavement. Dan quickly jumped off him and Birch came up holding his cheek, his pompadour in a mess.

"What the heck?" George said.

"He's a goddamn wrestler," Becker said. His palms were scraped and he was trying to brush the sand from the cuts.

"All go at once," George blurted.

When five of them moved in together, Dan turned and sprinted off. No one followed. The group stood around, speechless in their defeat. A few rubbed at sore spots.

They spent the rest of the night driving around the nearby roads, but Dan was not to be found. At a loss for what to do next, George sent a contingent to Dan's house. They broke down his mailbox and someone pissed on the door handle of his parents' car.

9

The first time she called, she asked the boy if he had seen George. When he said no, she said okay and hung up. The second time Colleen called, she said, "You seen George?"

"No," he said. "I think he's at the shop."

"I thought so."

"Why don't you call?"

"I don't want to talk to him," she said. "What are you doing?"

"Homework. Algebra."

"I hate math," she said.

"What are you doing?" he asked.

"Trying not to smoke cigarettes."

"You trying to quit?"

"Don't you ever just want to say, 'Screw it,' and get wicked fucked up?"

"I don't know. Sometimes."

"We should do it," she told him. "Just me and you, sneak off and get totally cocked."

"Yeah. Maybe."

"You're afraid of them."

"The guys?" he said.

"You shouldn't be," she said. "I bet you could take any of them."

"One's not the problem."

"You shouldn't let them tell you what to do."

"You do."

"I do it so I can be with George."

"I do it so I can hang out with them."

"Why?" she said.

"The politics—I don't know."

"I hate that crap the worst," Colleen said. "They just sit and talk. It's so boring."

He laughed.

"What?" she said.

"I'm surprised to hear you say that."

"I don't believe in any of their crap," she said.

"Then why are you with George?"

"I don't know. The way he talks. He's smart. He really listens. Sometimes."

He nodded. "I know what you mean."

"Listen, I have to go because my mom needs the phone, but you should call me," she said. "We should do what we talked about."

He hesitated and she hung up before he could answer.

The third time she called, sometime later in the week, she asked if he'd seen George, he said no, and she asked if she could come over to his house.

"Here?" he said.

"Yeah, I'm bored."

He'd never invited a girl over and he didn't know how his mother would react to this. He certainly didn't know how he could entertain Colleen because what he did know for sure was that his mother would insist upon the two remaining in some supervised space such as the living room or kitchen.

"My mother's home," he said.

"We don't have to stay."

Her answer relieved him.

"We could go to the mall," she said. "Let's go there."

He agreed, as this solution settled the problem of the mother. But as he hung up the phone he thought of the altogether separate and still unsolved dilemma of George Haney. It didn't necessarily rest upon him yet, though, for surely if this was merely two friends going to the mall, there was no dilemma.

During the drive, Colleen continued her habit of touching the boy. Her hand reached for him when not busy shifting the manual transmission. She stalled the car at a traffic light just before the mall entrance. "Fucking piece of shit," she said.

Her timing of clutch, stick, and accelerator had yet to be per-
fected, and often the car bucked in between gears. After
restarting the car, she revved the engine and popped the clutch,
making the tires spin weakly and scratch at the dry pavement.

Colleen drove around the outskirts of the mall and parked
in the back, outside one of the smaller department stores. She
looked at the boy, leaned over, and kissed him. It caught him
off guard, but the quick kiss didn't require much—he'd managed to slightly purse his lips before she got to him. She leaned
back to her side of the car, smiled, and got out. The dilemma
of George Haney had arrived. Inside the mall there were other
brief pecks here and there—slight taps of their lips together.
Since it was a weekday evening, the mall was nearly empty.

Colleen reached down and squeezed his hand. He squeezed
back, but he didn't look at her. She pulled him through a set of
doors, into a back hallway that led to some restrooms. She
leaned against a wall and pulled him close. She closed her eyes
and cocked her head to the side. He leaned in and pressed his
lips to hers. Her mouth opened and he felt her tongue slide between his lips. He opened his mouth and cautiously let his
tongue touch hers. She opened and closed her mouth ever so
slightly and he did his best to follow her lead. Just when he
thought he was getting the hang of it, Colleen opened her eyes
and pushed him back.

"You have to close your eyes," she said.

"Okay." He leaned in toward her, but her hand kept him at
bay.

"I'm not kidding," she said. "It's important."

"All right—I'll do it."

They closed their eyes and kissed again. He pressed his

body tightly to hers and Colleen did not shy from this friction. With her hands on the small of his back she pulled him tighter. He ran his hands over her breasts, but when he tried to slip his hand under her shirt, she stopped him.

"Nope," she said. "Sorry. Not here."

"Someplace else?" he said.

She smiled and shook her head. "You boys are all the same," she said, straightening her shirt. "Come on."

The comment confused him. Wasn't she the one who pulled him back there? And just how many boys was she basing this on? He knew he wasn't the first—with George and all—or even the second or third. He had heard what the guys said, that she and George often fought over the fact that she had slept with two guys from the punk-rock crowd before they got together.

As they strolled, he began to distance himself from her. Casually at first—he pulled his hand away from hers to yawn or stretch—then he moved out of range of her outstretched arm to look at something in a storefront window. Soon he ran out of polite maneuvers and his remove became obvious. Colleen didn't wait to respond. She stopped and grabbed his shirt.

"What's wrong?" She looked up at him with squinting, suspicious eyes. He shrugged at first and tried to turn away but Colleen held on to the handful of his shirt and turned him to face her.

"I don't know," he said. This was followed by another jolt to his shirt. "All right," he said, pulling her hand from its grip on him. "What about George?"

"What about him?"

"Yeah," he said. "What about him."

"I was with him—now I'm with you," she said.

The simplicity of it puzzled him. He doubted it could work out so neatly.

"They're going to kill me," he told her.

"It's not like you stole me," she said. "Me and George broke up two days ago."

This news was somewhat settling to the boy and momentarily it did seem as simple as she claimed: She had been with George, and now she was with him.

On the drive home, Colleen insisted on holding his hand, and when that became sweaty she placed her hand high on his thigh.

"Where do we go now?" she said. They were stopped at the traffic light at the end of the exit ramp into town.

"I live that way," he said, pointing east on the bypass.

"We're not done yet." Colleen smiled. She patted his thigh. "Where can we go?"

The only place he could think of was Woodbury Heights.

When the Escort pulled into the culvert at the end of the road, it parked amid charring and scars in the road. Black streaks of squealed tires and unskilled graffiti marred the pavement.

Colleen and the boy kissed and fondled each other for some time. He reached around her waist to the lever that controlled her seat. He pulled at it and leaned into her so that she was nearly flat. Before he could climb atop her, she stopped him, hands up, on his chest.

"We're not going to have sex," she said.

"Okay." He stopped and pulled away.

"Is that why you're here?" She paused. "Is it?" It was as if her affection had fled and turned to disgust.

"No," he said. He said nothing else, but seeing Colleen's unchanging face, he realized that nothing else would not suffice. "I care about you." He said it because it was the only thing he could think to say—the only thing he could think to say to make her like him again.

"Good," she said, suddenly smiling. She pulled him down to her so they could continue kissing. He felt a tinge of something, perhaps guilt—shame, maybe—but that feeling was lost when for the second time he slid his hand under her shirt and under her bra and this time she did not stop him. She let him undo the front of her pants and she let him touch her there. He shivered. He tried to ease her pants past her hips but she shook her head. She started to reach into his own trousers when a strange cramp gripped his abdomen. He winced and had to pull away.

"What?" she said.

"I don't know."

"What is it?"

"Nothing," he said. "My stomach's weird—I don't know."

"You're nervous," she told him.

He shook his head.

"It's cute," she said.

He bent back down to kiss her, but he heard something. Both of their heads jerked upright. A car was coming. He scrambled back toward his seat but he was only halfway there when the car passed. The engine raced and its tires squealed around the turn. He heard hollering over the rumble of the engine and recognized several of the local metalheads in the half-rusted muscle car. Terry Duvall sat in the front seat with his fist out the open window. Another hand protruded from the backseat, the middle finger raised at them. The boy ducked, fearing that if they saw him they might stop. When the car reached the far side of the culvert, he heard the engine thunder and the tires squeal. It was gone as fast as it had come.

"Jesus," Colleen said. Her head was crooked down, looking to button her pants. "Such assholes."

"They're all right," he said.

"They're idiots," she said.

He shook his head. "I grew up with them."

"If they're so great, why don't you hang out with them?"

The boy shrugged. He looked at her. One of her breasts, the one closer to him, was sandwiched between her raised shirt and her lowered bra. Once she finished with her pants, she dipped two fingers into her bra cup and pulled it out, allowing her breast to settle. Then she pulled her shirt down.

"Why not?" she said.

"I don't know," he said. "It's complicated."

Colleen sat and stared at him. "Tell me," she said.

After a moment, he started, "When I was getting questioned about the shooting, I told the cops some stuff that pissed Terry off."

"Did he get in trouble?"

He shook his head.

"So what's he mad about?"

"I don't know. It's complicated, I told you."

"It sounds stupid to me."

"Maybe I don't care what it sounds like to you."

"I didn't mean that you or him were stupid," she said. "I just meant the reason you guys are fighting seems stupid."

The boy sat silently, looking out the windshield of the car.

"What happened that day?" Colleen asked him.

"You know what happened. Kevin Dennison shot his brother by accident."

"I know I know that," she said. "But what happened?"

"I can't talk about it, I told you."

"Because of the investigation?"

He nodded.

"Will you tell me after it's over?"

"Why is it so important?"

Colleen shrugged. "It just seems important."

He shook his head. "Will you take me home?"

"Why?"

"I need to go," he said. "Take me home."

"Fine." Colleen started the car and the Escort bucked as she let out the clutch too quickly.

10

The following day the boy walked cautiously to the group of Youth members congregated around Jason Becker's Volkswagen in the school parking lot. He shook hands with a few and exchanged high-fives with a few others. He didn't sense any apprehension in their gestures. He couldn't make out any fury in their faces. It seemed impossible for them to know of his drive with Colleen, but still he worried. Espionage was at the heart of their role in the school. They listened.

After making his way to the center of the group and jovially punching fists with Jason Becker, he felt sure his secret was safe.

"The Wrench," Becker said.

"Hey, Becker," the boy said, smiling.

"You a good little boy in school today?"

"Always," he said.

Becker nodded.

The boy heard some hurried whispering from behind him. Becker craned his neck to look over his shoulder, then eased the boy aside and stepped past. The boy walked to the edge of the crowd to see who was drumming up the attention and he saw Kevin Dennison skulking across the lot. His pants were cuffed up to show off his black leather boots. A multitude of patches and safety-pinned scraps of material broke up the black of his backpack. Day by day Kevin seemed to grow further away from the prep-school image he'd once had. The boy had passed Kevin one day at his locker and come close enough to read the patches on his backpack. The one that stuck with him said TOO DRUNK TO FUCK.

Before getting to his car, Kevin turned and looked at the mob of staring Youth. He squinted his eyes and bobbed a middle finger in the air between them.

"Fuck you, faggot!" someone in the group shouted.

"Come on over here, you pussy," someone else yelled.

"Hey, Dennison," Becker shouted. Kevin didn't look up from unlocking the door of his car. "Why don't you smoke a dick instead of all those joints?"

At that the group fell into laughter. One after another they reached high-fives out to Jason Becker. He smiled and clapped the hands above him in the air. Kevin got in his car and left without looking back.

"Think he knows?" Birch said.

"That burnout?" said Becker. "He doesn't know his head from his ass."

The excitement of the group waned and they began mulling about in smaller, separate conversations. The boy made his way back over to Becker's side.

"What's up?" the boy said.

"What's up with what, my man?"

"With Dennison." The boy pointed a thumb back to where Kevin had been parked.

"I thought George had filled you in." Becker put his arm around him and pulled him close. "You're especially going to love this. Thing is, we found out Mr. Dennison's been peddling a little grass at the Coffee House. And this is the sweet part: We know he keeps it on him, and that he keeps it all wrapped separately." He threw a jab at the boy and smiled.

The boy didn't smile back.

"That's 'intent to distribute,'" Jason said. "That's deep shit. We're going to keep an eye on the Coffee House. If he's there this weekend, George is going to call it in. It's going to be killer—we're going to videotape it from across the street."

"You going to the Haneys' shop?" the boy said.

"In a bit."

"Can I come?"

"Sure. What's up?"

"Nothing," the boy said. "I need to talk to George."

George stared at the boy from behind the counter and the boy stared back.

"This junkie tried to ruin your life and now you want to help him?" George said.

"You can't do it," said the boy.

"The fuck we can't," Becker said.

"He didn't try to ruin my life."

"I'd say shooting his brother in your home and trying to pin it on you is pretty close," George said.

"It was an accident."

"I don't give a damn," Becker said. "The kid's a drug dealer. Period."

"I'll talk to him," the boy said.

"The hell you will." Becker leaned in close to the boy.

"Easy, Jason," George said. "Back off."

The boy looked at Becker. "Yeah," he said.

"What?" Becker said. "Who is this tough guy?"

"Jason," George snapped. He pointed at the door. "Take a walk."

Becker stared at him.

"I can't have a conversation with you like this." George pointed again at the door. Jason glared at the boy but did as he was told. The door boomed behind him as he barged out.

"There," George said.

"Yeah," the boy said. "There."

"Ted, we're doing this for you."

The boy shook his head. "I don't want you to."

"I know," George said. "But I don't get it. This could turn the investigation in your favor."

"His brother died."

"So we should pardon every criminal with a good excuse?" George said. "Every thief who grew up poor? Every prostitute who was abused?"

"You guys break the law," the boy said. "Tearing up people's stuff."

"They deserve it."

"Just because you say so," said the boy. "Just because you make it up."

"I don't make anything up," George told him. "We're working for a greater good, for a greater law. We can't let sentimentality sway us, Ted. Mr. Dennison must be punished. Case closed."

"I don't think I can let you do it."

"Then I'm afraid that we'll have to deal with you too."

"Fine," the boy said. He turned to leave.

"Teddy."

The boy stopped.

"Please think about this. We make better friends than enemies."

"I know," the boy said. He paused. "I will." He walked out the door and across the lot to the side of the bypass. Jason Becker leaned against his car, leering at the boy. He didn't look at Jason. He walked down the side of the bypass toward home. He turned and stuck out his thumb each time a car passed. An old man in a Chevy pickup finally slowed and stopped. The boy jogged to catch up and hopped in the cab. They greeted each other but spoke little more than that.

The boy thought about Kevin. It made sense to let the Youth have their way. Kevin's arrest would reflect poorly upon him. Perhaps the investigators would look more favorably upon his own story after seeing what Kevin was capable of.

The old man stopped at the corner of his street. The boy

thanked him, hopped out, and walked the rest of the way home. Shortly after he arrived, the phone rang. He hesitated to pick it up, but on the fourth ring he pulled the phone from its cradle.

"Ted," his Uncle John said. "How are you?"

The boy was relieved. "Fine. You?"

"Got any plans this evening?"

"Some homework."

"Got time to give me a hand with a deer? Skin and quarter it?" John said. "I'd let it hang but it's so warm I got to get it in the fridge."

"Season's open already?"

"Opened this week," John said.

"You want me to ride my bike over?"

"Nah," John said. "Get your father's good cutlery. I'll be there in ten minutes."

"Sure," the boy said. "See you."

He hung up the phone and ran upstairs to change. Then he went to the basement and rifled through a box of his father's hunting gear. He found the two knives he was looking for, pulled them from their sheaths, and ran a finger along their blades. He grabbed a stone from the box and small bottle of oil and went to the workbench. He laid out the stone and oiled it. He started with the skinning knife, slowly drawing the rounded blade along the stone, alternating from one side to the other. He touched the blade again and his thumb instinctively jumped back. Satisfied, he set to the longer, more slender blade of the boning knife.

He waited in the driveway for his uncle. Once at John's house, they walked around back to a small shed and John lifted a two-by-four from the yoke between the doors. One side swung open. A rope from a rafter was noosed around the deer's neck and held it upright in the shed.

"Nice deer," the boy said. "Six-point."

"Five," the uncle told him. "Other side's only got two."

"Healthy," the boy said. He ran a hand down the soft, shiny coat. The deer was thick in the midsection and good and wide across the hindquarters. "Where'd you get him?"

The uncle smiled and held a finger to his lips. He pointed a finger out in the direction behind the house. The Darling property extended from behind the boy's house all the way over the hill and abutted the uncle's land.

"Poacher," the boy said, smiling.

"Nobody knows any different," John said. He took a hacksaw from a nail on the side of the shed. "Want to get ahold of him for me?"

The boy nodded and grabbed the deer to keep it from swinging on the rope. John took a hoof and ran the saw back and forth through the leg at the knee. The sound wasn't pleasant, but the boy had grown accustomed to it. John threw each leg in a corner and hung the saw back on the wall. He took out his knife and ran it around the deer's neck, just behind the ears, just deep enough to cut the hide. Then he cut the hide down the throat and chest to the opening in the carcass at the bottom of the sternum. They each took a corner of the hide and began to pull it away from the body, carefully running a blade along the fissure between muscle and skin.

After they cut the skin away from the front legs and pulled it back behind the shoulders, they put their knives down. They each took ahold of the fur and put their weight into it. The hide pulled away from the carcass with a hiss. They skinned the hind legs and hacked off the bone that connected the tail. The deer hung naked, the muscle red and purple, the rump thick with white fat. John took the skin and hung it over the back of a sawhorse.

The boy took hold of the deer again as the uncle set to the tenderloins on the inside of the lower back. The muscle was still warm. Without the fur, the boy could see where the arrow had punctured the rib cage just behind the shoulder. It was a textbook shot, the broadhead probably puncturing the heart or lungs. Death came fast, as the blood quickly pooled inside.

The boy allowed his hand to slide down from the deer's shoulder. He ran his finger around the entrance wound. It was black at the edges, where the blood had clotted. He dipped the tip of his finger into the hole and felt the dried, hardened flesh, the sharp edge of bone. He closed his eyes. In the darkness he saw Bobby, noosed and naked, and the boy's finger dipped into the hole in Bobby's chest. His eyes popped open and his hands jumped back from the deer. The carcass swung away from his uncle.

"Hey," John said, looking around the deer.

"Sorry," he said. "I had an itch." He took hold of the deer again and John finished with the second tenderloin. He laid it on a small tray beside the first. He cut into the meat of the lower back, all the way to the spine on either side.

"You want to catch?" John said.

"Huh?"

"I'll cut, you catch?" John said. "You all right?"

The boy nodded.

"You sure?"

He nodded again and crouched next to the animal. He got a good grip on the hindquarters and John set to the spine with the hacksaw. The boy wobbled under the weight when the saw cleared the bone and John helped him carry it inside. They separated the hindquarters and set each side in the bottom of a refrigerator in the basement. They went to the shed and returned with the two front shoulders. They cut down the torso and cut out the chops, the neck, and the belly meat. They stacked the cuts in the refrigerator.

"That's all?" the boy said.

John nodded. "I want to age it some," he said. "I'll get to it this weekend."

He took the knives and the cutting board they had used to a large sink in the corner to begin the cleanup. The boy looked at the rib cage on the table. With the chops cut away, the spine ran like a tall, narrow mohawk down the center. He walked over and looked again at the entry wound. With the flesh cut away, it looked small and hardly seemed capable of bringing the animal down. The boy ran a finger back and forth over the opening. The heat had dissipated and it was cool to the touch.

"What the heck is wrong with you tonight?"

The boy flinched and saw that John was watching him from across the room. "Nothing," he told his uncle.

"Come on," John said. "You're stumbling around here like a zombie. What's up?"

The boy shrugged. "I got to decide something."

"What about?"

"Remember Kevin Dennison?" the boy said.

"Kind of a tough one to forget."

"He's selling pot. And some guys I know want to rat him out."

"What's the choice you got?"

"I could tell him or not," the boy said. "What they're going to do."

"Why would you?"

"It doesn't seem right," the boy said. "To get him in more trouble."

"More?" John said.

"You know, more than we're already in."

"I'm going to ask you something and I don't want you to take it the wrong way."

The boy looked at his uncle.

"You shoot that kid? That brother of his?"

"No," the boy said. "Hell no. Why?"

The uncle shrugged. "Something about it doesn't sit right with me."

"I didn't shoot him," the boy said. "I swear."

"All right," John told him. "Take it easy—I believe you."

The boy looked at the floor. "I loaded the gun," he said. He looked up at his uncle.

John nodded. "Why aren't you telling the truth?"

"Ma says we could get sued and lose everything," he said. "You can't tell her I told you. You can't."

"I won't say anything," John told him. "But I will tell you something about your mother."

"What?"

"Our father," he said. "When we were kids, a terrible drunk. Sober, he was straight as the Pope, but get a couple drinks in him and he was a twisted son of a bitch. Mean, I'm telling you, a real ball-breaker. And your mother," John said. "She was the type who could wake up the morning after one of his nights and go to school with a smile on her face like nothing happened. Hell, she'd have a story explaining the bruise on the side of my head before we got to the breakfast table. Me, I tried, believe me." He looked at the boy and the boy nodded. "I don't know what type you are," John said. "But I'll tell you, it ain't about the law. It's about how something sits with you. Your guts won't always say when you're doing right, but they know sure as shit when you're doing wrong. I believe that, Ted. That's why I ain't going to tell you what to do. I know you know."

The boy nodded. "You won't tell?" he said.

John shook his head.

"Thanks," the boy said.

"Long as you don't repeat what I told you."

"I won't," the boy said. He smiled and John smiled back.

"Come on," John said. "Let's get you home."

The following day the boy walked cautiously through school. He knew the Youth were keeping a close eye on him. He saw them about, eyeing him, waiting for him to make his move, waiting for some indication of treachery. But they kept their distance and he kept his. He realized he was running out of time. It was Friday and he knew the Youth would try to make their move over the weekend.

He saw Kevin twice in school and both times his heart started to race and his breathing quickened. He was afraid of the Youth but he was also terribly afraid of Kevin—he had been since the day he lied. It was because of that lie that the boy knew he couldn't let the Youth turn Kevin in. But it was also that lie that made approaching Kevin impossible. What could he possibly say to him? And if he called, what would he do if Mrs. Dennison picked up the phone?

In English class, he stared at the blank page in his notebook. Mr. O'Shea gave them the last five or ten minutes of class to free-write in their journals. The boy thought about reflecting on "Ode on a Grecian Urn," as O'Shea had suggested, but he didn't get the poem in the least. He listened to the scratch of pens against paper as the students around him scribbled away. He took up his pen and started in the top left corner of the page:

Kevin,

They know you are selling drugs. They know you do it at the Coffee House. They are going to call the cops. They are going to videotape it from across the street. You know who they are. Please don't get caught.

A Friend

O'Shea gave him a dirty look when he tore the page out of his notebook. They were supposed to keep their journal writings together over the course of the quarter. The boy shrugged, folded the paper, and tucked it into his pocket. Neither O'Shea nor grades was high on his list of priorities.

After the bell rang, the boy made his way into the surge of students in the hall. He moved with the tide of bodies and kept an eye out for Youth members. He went to a water fountain and ducked his head for a drink. He stood and looked either way. His next class was in the science wing, but he took a quick turn toward the gym. He knew he was taking a chance even being seen near Kevin's locker; he was sure the Youth knew where it was. Before he got there he pulled the note out of his pocket, and as he passed, he slipped it through the vent at the top of the metal door. He walked to the end of the hallway and turned around, heading back in the direction of his next class.

When he turned the corner toward the science wing, he saw Colleen standing down the hall, leaning against the wall with her arms crossed. He wanted to take another turn, a quick detour around her, but he saw that she saw him.

"Hey," he said when he arrived before her.

"Why are you avoiding me?" she said.

"I'm not."

"I saw you turn back there, down the other hall."

He shook his head. "It's not what you think," he told her.

"I can talk to George," she said. "I'll make it okay."

"No." He shook his head. "No you won't."

"So you want to pretend that we aren't even dating?"

"We've only been on one date."

"Fine," she said.

"You want to go out this weekend?"

"I don't think so. I think I'm busy."

"Fine," said the boy.

The two turned and walked in opposite directions in the hallway.

11

He spent an uneventful weekend by himself, anxious about what the coming week would bring. On Monday, he was relieved when the Youth members he saw smiled and acted warmly toward him. Birch even gave him a quick pat on the back on his way by in the hallway. But underneath the relief, he also felt a bit of remorse, perhaps even sadness. If the Youth were happy, their plot to bring down Kevin Dennison must have gone as planned. Maybe the note had been lost in Kevin's locker. Or maybe Kevin never returned to it on Friday afternoon.

Peckerhead was late coming into third-period biology and

he was also quick to leave. The boy grew uneasy and his sus-
picions heightened when Peckerhead disappeared after their
last-period American government class. He walked alone
down the hallway of the portable and squinted as he stepped
out into the bright fall sun. He headed across the cement
courtyard to the front of the school, where the buses idled. It
seemed safest to head home. Perhaps he could probe the
Youth with a few phone calls that evening.

He was halfway across the courtyard when he saw Jason
Becker and Birch coming his way. He was about to put his
head down and make a jog for the bus, but they both smiled.
Becker even waved. The boy slowed so that their paths inter-
sected.

"Teddy," Birch said, holding his fist out.

The boy punched at it.

Becker gave him a quick, playful shove. "The Wrench," he
said. "What are you doing?"

"Nothing," he said.

"Heading home?" Birch said, looking in the direction of
the buses.

The boy nodded. "I got homework," he said.

"Nah," Jason said. "Come with us." He smiled and shoved
him again.

"Yeah?" the boy said.

"Don't be a dumb-ass." Jason smiled and walked in the direction of the parking lot. The boy fell in behind them.

When they got to the parking lot, something in the boy told
him to run. It felt wrong. The usual crowd wasn't there, no
George, no Peckerhead, no mob of young cadets. He looked

back over his shoulder and saw the last two buses groaning out of the drive.

"Where is everyone?" he said.

"At the shop," Birch told him. "We're all meeting up there."

Becker climbed into the driver's seat of the Volkswagen and Birch held the passenger door open for him. The front seat was folded forward, but the boy hesitated. Becker bent his neck down to look at him.

"Come on," he said.

The boy didn't move.

"What choice you got?" said Birch. "You going to walk?"

The boy got into the backseat.

"That a boy," Becker said, smiling. Once they were in the flow of traffic, Becker looked over his shoulder. "Everyone's at the shop to watch the video from this weekend."

The boy looked down at his lap. His hands played with a torn corner of nylon that hung from the seat in front of him.

"Cool," he said. He smiled quickly, but then he winced, thinking of how he had failed Kevin again.

When they arrived at the shop, he saw Colleen's car in the lot. He walked through the door, and it wasn't the mob of Youth members that surprised him. It wasn't the television on the counter or the ring of chairs set up around it. The quiet looks on their faces didn't catch his attention. What struck him when he entered the shop was the sight of Colleen Crenshaw standing at George's side, behind the glass case of handguns and knives. Her hand was flat on the counter and his was atop hers. George's eyes were upon him as soon as he entered the store, but Colleen looked down, away, anywhere but in his direction.

"Glad you could make it, Theodore," George said.

The boy nodded.

"Take a seat," George told him, but he didn't move.

"Please," George said, motioning to the chairs before the television.

When the boy still didn't budge, Becker took him by an elbow and walked him across the room.

"Sit," Becker said, and the boy sat.

"We have a little something we'd like you to see," George said. He reached over the top of the counter and turned on the television. It erupted in static. He pushed a tape into the VCR and the television went quiet, the snow on the screen replaced by a night shot of the local coffeehouse. A girl walked out holding a foam coffee cup. The boy heard whispering in the background of the video. The camera panned down the sidewalk and came to rest on three boys standing by a car in the parking lot. When the camera zoomed in, the boy recognized one of them as Kevin Dennison. The three leaned in to speak privately. Then they all leaned back and laughed. Kevin buckled over, holding his guts. One of his friends held a hand over his face and leaned back on a car. They seemed stoned out of their minds. The boy grew nauseous thinking where it was all headed.

One of Kevin's friends stepped behind a car for a moment and then he walked down the sidewalk toward the entrance. He had a black hooded sweatshirt on that hung past his waist.

Halfway to the entrance he bobbled his empty coffee cup and dropped it. When he bent over to grab it, his bare ass popped out from under his sweatshirt. It happened so quickly that the boy doubted what he'd seen. The kid got to the entrance, threw out his cup in a trash can, and returned to his friends in the parking lot. The three laughed wildly. There was silence in the room around the boy.

"What the fuck?" someone whispered on the videotape.

Kevin regained his composure and headed down the sidewalk. He was stiff, unnaturally upright. He stopped, looked down, and quickly bent over as if to tie his shoe. His pale ass blinked out from under his untucked shirt. He stood, but held his shirt up and slapped his ass. Then he pulled up his pants and turned to face the camera. He bobbed two middle fingers up and down and turned it into a kind of dance, gyrating, turning, flipping the camera off the entire time. When he finished his dance, he faced the camera again and pulled out the insides of his pockets. Then he smiled and held his hands up in a mocking shrug. The two other boys quickly ran over and began to moon the camera again. The boy was entranced by the footage. He wanted to laugh and cheer for them, but the screen went back to static.

George reached over the counter and turned off the television. No one spoke. The boy could hear the many Youth members shifting their weight on the creaky floor around him. He tried to steady his breathing and he wiped his hands along the legs of his pants.

"So," George said. "We have been humiliated." He walked out from behind the counter. "And I can only assume it was possible because of you, Theodore."

The boy looked at George. He thought through his options.

"But this isn't the end of the world," George said to him. "We all make mistakes. And with the proper amount of repentance, we can all be forgiven. At the end of the day, Theodore, we want you on our side."

The boy knew he could grovel and beg his way back into their favor. But he looked at the group around him—their khakis and loafers, their goddamn argyle socks. He looked at Colleen, behind the counter, picking at a fingernail. She looked up quickly and he caught her eye. She blinked slowly. She saw George watching her and she went back to working at her finger.

"Are you even going to try to deny it?" George asked him.

"Does it matter?" the boy said. He thought of Kevin and his two friends. He thought of Terry Duvall and Dan the wrestler. He looked quickly at the door and saw that he had a clear alley.

"Of course it does," George said. "Did you tell him, Theodore?"

"Don't call me that," he said. He reached up and scratched his head. Then he lurched out of the folding chair and sprinted for the exit. He felt the tug of someone grabbing his shirt, but the tension quickly gave way. He hit the horizontal bar of the door at full stride and blew it open. It slowed him a bit and gave them the time they needed. He felt a hard kick to his trailing leg, which sent his foot colliding into his opposite heel. Tripped up at the top of three stairs, he had nowhere to go but down. He got his hands out in front of him, but they hardly slowed his fall. He came to the ground with a grunt and the clash of his teeth. A blast of white light flashed inside his clenched eyes. He bounced and slid to a stop in the rocky dirt of the drive.

He rolled over and immediately clasped a hand over his mouth. His tongue had been between his teeth. He couldn't feel it and he feared he had bitten it off. He opened his mouth and touched the tip. It was still there, but his fingers came away thick with blood. He looked up at the group of awestruck boys. Peckerhead cringed and turned away.

The boy grabbed a baseball-size rock and clambered to his feet. He stayed low, the rock back and ready. He felt like an animal. He knew he would swing the stone with all his might at anyone who approached and the Youth seemed to sense this. The boy felt the warm fluid dripping off his chin. He took a couple of steps back and wiped at his face. There was more of his blood than he'd ever seen. He spat at his feet and it came out crimson and bubbly. He tried to threaten them. He tried to tell them he would kill anyone who so much as stepped a foot closer, but it came out garbled and meaningless. He continued to back up, step by step. He saw another good-size rock at his feet and he grabbed it with his empty hand. He shook it at them.

As he backed past a parked car, the tingling in his mouth began to turn into a searing pain. The superhuman strength he felt, the fearlessness, was melting from his limbs. He leaned against the car. He shook the rocks at the boys another time and then turned and sat, his back resting against the tire. He kept the rocks tight in his fists and listened carefully for footsteps. He spat again at his side and at the sight of the blood he realized the fear was coming fast. What if he'd done something they couldn't fix? What if he couldn't speak again?

"Teddy?" George called out.

The boy grunted. He jumped to his feet and hurled one of his stones. The group scattered and the rock bashed into the vinyl siding of the shop. The boy shook his second stone before turning and sitting again.

"Ted," George hollered. "What is wrong with you? Come on out of there so we can get you to the hospital."

The boy shook his rock above the fender of the car for everyone to see.

"This isn't at all what we wanted, Ted," George went on, but the boy was shrinking back inside his head. He was filled with a terrible fury. He wanted to beat them all to pulp. Even more, he wanted to dash in his own head—take the sharp end of the rock and go for his temple, over and over again, until the job was done. He was furious with himself for being so desperate, for needing their company, for believing Colleen. He hated this bleeding, whimpering thing he'd become, hiding like a child behind this car. Tears began to run down his cheeks, and they only added to his rage.

"Ted?" Colleen's voice drew him back. "Please don't throw a rock at me, okay? It's just me. I'm going to pull my car over there and we're going to go to the hospital. Okay?"

He fisted the rock until the edges began to cut into his hand. He wanted to kick her until she wept. He heard her car start and shift. He heard her back out and pull forward in his direction. He wiped fiercely at his face to hide the tears. The Escort pulled up beside him and she leaned over and threw open the door. He didn't move.

"Come on," she said. She waved him into the front seat.

He still didn't budge. He glared at her out of the corner of his eye.

"It's either me or them," she said.

He slowly got to his feet and walked to the car. He never looked back at the group of boys in the lot.

"How bad is it?" Colleen said.

He flinched when she reached across the car but she only went for the visor above the windshield and pulled it down.

"Do you want to look?" she said

He saw himself in the mirror. Blood was smeared across his cheek and jawline. Fresh drops ran down from the corners of his mouth. His eyes were runny and bloodshot. He slowly opened his mouth. At first it didn't seem too bad. A cut ran halfway across his tongue. But when he stuck it out of his mouth, the weight of the hanging tip pulled the wound open. He saw the raw meat of the deep cut and drew it back in. He closed his eyes and cringed. He shook his head.

"Bad?" she said.

He nodded.

"I'm so sorry, Ted," she said.

He told her to fuck off.

She leaned closer. "Huh?" she said.

He shook his head. He batted a hand that told her to forget about it. He put his face in his hands and leaned over against the door.

"Back there," she said. "It wasn't what it looked like."

He didn't move.

"When I heard what they were going to do, I went to George to try to stop him," she said. "I thought if I was there they wouldn't hurt you."

He shook his head. "Fanks," he said.

"I'm serious," she said.

He held up a hand for her to stop talking. She did.

At the hospital they sat before the registry desk. When the woman returned, she had several packets of large gauze pads. She helped the boy open them and he used the first couple to wipe his face. He spit a mouthful of blood into the next handful and held a couple more over his mouth.

"Okay," she said. "Let's get some paperwork done so we can get you in to see someone."

He nodded.

"You can't talk?" she said.

He shook his head.

"This will do," she said. She took a prescription pad off her desk and a pen out of a coffee mug and handed them both to the boy. She asked him questions and he wrote out the answers.

"How did the injury occur?" she said.

He wrote, *Fell*.

"He fell?" she said to Colleen.

Colleen nodded. "He tripped at the top of a couple stairs," she said.

The woman behind the desk nodded. "You're under eighteen? Do you have a number where we can reach your parents?"

He wrote down his home number and the woman dialed it. She held the phone to her head but eventually shook her head. "No answer," she said.

He scratched a second number on the pad and wrote, *Ask for Donna LeClare.*

The woman dialed and asked for his mother. "It's an emergency," she said. After a long wait she introduced herself and explained the situation to his mother. "We'd like to get him in to a doctor as soon as possible. He can't talk at the moment. He has a friend here with him. Would you mind giving me consent before I do that? Yes, I think it's important that he's seen immediately. Okay. Yes. Thank you. Here's his friend." She handed the phone over to Colleen and came around the end of the desk. "Come with me, Teddy," she said.

He followed her through a set of swinging doors, down a hall, and into one of many small rooms.

"Climb right up there on the bed," she said. "Someone will be in shortly."

He sat with his head in his hands and then leaned back and pulled his legs up on the bed. He let an arm fall across his face to hide his eyes from the bright fluorescent lights. There was a quick knock on the door before it opened. A smiling Indian man in a white coat stepped through the door, a younger woman following.

"Mr. LeClare," he said. "I hear we had a run-in with some stairs."

The boy nodded and he began to sit up, but the doctor was already at his side with a warm, heavy hand on his chest. The woman stayed back, just behind him.

"You can stay," he told the boy. He had him rest his head on the pillow and he ran his hands over his jaw and neck, pressing and probing the bone and muscle. "Any pain when I do this?" he said.

The boy shook his head.

"Lose consciousness at all?"

He shook his head again.

"See any stars or bright flashes?"

He shrugged.

"Yes?" the doctor said. "Sounds like you took a pretty good hit."

The boy smiled.

"Okay," the doctor said. "Now let's get a look at that tongue." He went across the room and came back with a wooden tongue depressor. He had him open his mouth and he moved his tongue around with the wooden depressor and his gloved fingers. "Looks like the stairs won this round," he said. The woman looked over his shoulder. "But I think we'll live to fight another day." He listed off the things he would need to the woman and she wrote them down on a clipboard.

"I'll be right back," he said to the boy. "And we'll get you stitched up." He smiled and stepped through the door.

There was another knock, but this time Colleen poked her head through. She smiled when she saw him. She walked over and sat on the chair beside his bed. She looked down at him and ran a hand up his chest and along his cheek, dragging her fingernails across his scalp. He closed his eyes and focused on the feeling. She reached back and massaged his neck.

"Sorry I took so long," she said. "Your mother had a ton of questions. She'll be here soon."

The door opened and Colleen took her hand away. The boy opened his eyes and saw the woman who had come in with the doctor. She had a tray of odds and ends that she placed on the table beside the bed.

The doctor was close behind her. He adjusted the height of

a wheeled stool and folded the railing of the bed down. He situated himself above the boy and arranged the things on the tray beside him.

"Do you mind if I stay?" Colleen said.

"Not at all," the doctor said. "I only ask that if you have a soft spot for blood or needles or anything of the sort that you look away and stay seated. I don't need another patient." He smiled and Colleen smiled back.

"Okay," she said.

"Now, Ted," the doctor said. "This is going to be a bit like the dentist. Ever had Novocain?"

The boy nodded.

"I'm going to give you a couple injections of something like it. And it's going to burn like a son of a gun. But after that you shouldn't feel much of anything. Sound all right?"

The boy shrugged. He felt Colleen take his hand in both of hers. When he saw the doctor reaching in with the needle, he opened his mouth and closed his eyes. A heavy hand fell on his chin and then it felt as if the doctor were pushing a red-hot needle into his tongue. He bore down on Colleen's hand and arched his back against the bed.

"A few more spots and we'll be done," the doctor said. "You're doing great."

The boy felt the needle withdraw and plunge again and again. Each time he had to fight the urge to clamp his jaw shut. His hand grew hot and sweaty in Colleen's.

"Now we're just going to give the medicine a chance to work," the doctor said.

The boy nodded. He opened his eyes and looked over at Colleen. She had her forehead down on the back of her hand that held his. He looked back to the doctor. The doctor smiled. The boy noticed that his tongue had begun to disappear.

After a moment the doctor was back in his mouth. The boy felt the pressure of his tongue being held in place. When he saw the doctor draw the needle up to pull the suture tight, he felt the tug, tug, tug of the string on his tongue.

The doctor prescribed an oral antibiotic and an antiseptic mouthwash. He told the boy that the stitches would dissolve on their own and that he didn't need to return unless something went wrong. He said the swelling should go down in a day or so and he told the boy that Popsicles would help. The doctor smiled when he said *Popsicles*.

The boy shook his hand and left the room. He waited for Colleen, then headed down the hall toward the waiting room. He saw his mother at the opposite end, but she didn't see him. She walked quickly, her purse under her arm. She ducked her head as if to go faster. The boy stayed in her path. When she looked up to see the obstruction, she was startled to see it was him.

"Goodness," she said. She put an open hand on her chest. "Already done?"

The boy smiled, amused with himself for surprising her. He nodded.

"Let me see," she said. She reached and took him by the chin, pushing his mouth gently open. He stuck his tongue out. "Ouch," she said. "Hurt?"

He shrugged.

"You fell?" his mother said.

He nodded.

"He tripped at the top of a couple stairs," Colleen said.

"Thanks for being here with him, Colleen."

Colleen smiled and nodded.

"My boy must be growing," the mother said. "He's getting clumsy." She smiled at the both of them.

The boy held out the two prescriptions and his mother took them.

"We can pick these up on the way home," she said.

"The doctor also said Popsicles would help with the swelling," Colleen said.

"Popsicles it is, then," the mother said. They headed down the hall.

"Mrs. LeClare?" Colleen said. "Do you mind if I come over?"

"No," the mother said. "If your parents don't mind."

"No one's home," Colleen said. "I get creeped out by myself."

"I'm sure Teddy would like the company."

The boy looked at Colleen and shook his head. He wanted to ask her who the hell she thought she was, inviting herself over to his house. He wanted to tell her to go on back to George and his little study group. He wanted to explain to her just how upset seeing her with George had made him, but all that was impossible with his tongue as useless as it was. He could only frown and shake his head.

Colleen playfully slapped at his forearm and followed him out of the hospital.

Colleen and the mother ate bacon, lettuce, and tomato sandwiches on toasted white bread while the boy sucked on a milk-

shake that his mother made. After dinner she went upstairs to
grade student work while he and Colleen sat on the couch and
watched television. After some time Colleen pulled his head
down to her lap. He put his feet up and rested his head on her
thigh. She ran her fingers through his hair and massaged his
scalp.

At a commercial break he got up to use the bathroom.
When he returned, he saw that Colleen was sprawled across
the couch. Rather than sitting back up, she opened her arms
for him. He paused for a moment and then lay beside her, letting his head rest against her warm, soft chest. She kissed his
forehead and ran her hand up his back, under his shirt. He
closed his eyes and felt his breathing go slow and heavy.

Sometime later he heard movement upstairs. He untangled
himself from Colleen and sat up.

"Teddy?" his mother called down. "Ted?"

He grunted.

"I think it's time for Colleen to head home."

"Okay, Mrs. LeClare," Colleen said. "Thank you for dinner."

"Glad to have you," the mother said. "Have a good week
at school."

"You too, Mrs. LeClare."

On the front steps outside the house, Colleen ran her hand
up and down his chest. She kissed him on the lips. "Good
night baby," she said.

He nodded and smiled.

After she'd backed out and headed down the road, he went
inside. He turned off the television and the lights on the first
floor, then walked up the stairs to say good night to his mother.

In the bathroom he stuck out his tongue in the mirror. It was swollen and discolored. The black stitches wound like a helix through either side of the cut. He brushed his teeth and rinsed with the antiseptic mouthwash. He winced at the pain. He killed the light in the bathroom and walked across the hall to his room.

Undressed and under the covers, he didn't think of Bobby or the investigation. He didn't think of George and the Youth. He thought of the warm feeling that had filled him in Colleen's arms. He thought of the searing pain that had filled his mouth earlier in the day. Sleep came fast.

The following day in school, he carried around a sheet of paper. It said, *I have stitches in my tongue. I can't talk. Thanks for understanding.* After he handed each teacher the note, he opened his mouth as proof. When the teacher asked how it happened, he flipped the paper over. There it said, *I fell.*

By the end of the week the swelling was gone and the cut had begun to close. Still the boy chose not to talk. He liked the silence. It allowed him to stay back, behind his eyes, where it was quiet and less complicated.

The Youth stayed out of his way for a spell. Whether they were sympathetic to his injury or fearful of his rock-wielding rage, the boy did not know.

12

At the end of the following week, Colleen's sister and her husband invited Colleen and the boy over for the evening, for drinks. The boy had never been anywhere for drinks. Sure, he'd gone places *to* drink—the gravel pits and basements about town—but this was different. *For drinks* sounded sophisticated. He knew he was breaking Youth doctrine, but hell, he was messing around with Colleen and he'd already ruined the Youth plot against Kevin Dennison. Really, the boy thought, what was a couple of drinks?

When they arrived, Colleen's nephew was hanging in a swinging chair and her sister was spooning food into his mouth. Jenny was a rounder, lighter-haired version of Colleen. She greeted them, placing the jar of baby food on the coffee table to shake the boy's hand. Jenny told them to make themselves comfortable. She said she'd be done in a minute. When her husband, Doug, came into the room, the boy was surprised at how young he looked. He gave them a weak smile.

"Get drinks," Jenny told Doug. And Doug went to get drinks. "Daiquiris," Jenny said. And Doug made daiquiris— strawberry, frozen, from a can in the freezer.

"You want some of this?" Doug asked him, holding up the blender pitcher. "I've got beers," Doug added. He nodded and Doug handed two mugs of daiquiris to Colleen and Jenny, went to the fridge, and came back with two cans of Budweiser. He handed one to the boy. "Only the best," Doug said.

"Cheers," said Jenny, and the four leaned in and clicked their drinks together.

It wasn't long until several rounds had gone down and Doug was sent back into the kitchen for another batch of frozen cocktails.

Jenny said, "Piña coladas," and Doug made piña coladas with another can of frozen mix. "I'm so glad you're not with that . . ." Jenny took a sip off the top of her new cocktail. "That Nazi." She looked at Colleen. The two of them were giddy with drink. "You're not into that no-drinking, no-drugs, no-sex thing, are you, Ted?" She reached out to her son's swing and gave it a light push.

The boy shook his head and held up his most recent Budweiser with a smile. He was feeling the alcohol as well.

"That's good," Jenny said. "Good for Colleen, anyway." She pointed at her sister and laughed out loud.

"Shut up," said Colleen.

"Serious, though." Jenny stopped laughing. "George and those guys are just weird."

The boy smiled and raised the beer to his lips. He finished the last quarter of the can.

"All right," Jenny said. "Part of the deal is that you guys have to watch Jimmy while me and Doug go and check on some friends." She gently rubbed her son's head with one hand and her other hand shot up with the empty glass in it. Doug retrieved the glass and filled it with what was left in the pitcher. With her drink full, Jenny took Doug's hand and pulled him toward the door.

"Adiós," Doug said.

"We'll knock," said Jenny through the closing gap of the door. "Take care of my baby," she said at the last second. Colleen chuckled and looked at the boy. He shrugged.

"They're going to smoke pot," Colleen said. "They have friends two floors up. They'll be a while."

He smiled.

"I do it sometimes," she said. "You?"

"I tried it," he said. "Didn't get anything off it, though."

"We'll do it," she said. "Me and you. We'll get totally stoned."

He leaned forward to put his beer on the coffee table. When he returned to the couch, he slid over, close to Colleen. He put his arm around her and she leaned into him. When she looked up at him, he kissed her.

"I couldn't wait for them to leave," she said.

She kissed him back, thrusting her tongue into his mouth. His own tongue was still a bit tender, but he managed to flop it about as the kissing required. After waiting for what he thought was an appropriate time, he ran a hand over one of her breasts. She rubbed the crotch of his jeans. When she leaned back, he followed her.

"Take off your shoes," she said.

He hesitated.

"It's a new sofa," she told him.

He sat up and slid off his loafers. Colleen smiled and kicked her feet up and down on the couch. He untied her sneakers and pulled them off, tossing them to the floor. She looked back, above her head, and gave the swing her nephew sat in a gentle push.

The boy lay upon her and they kissed. He pushed her shirt up to her armpits and fussed with her bra until she laughed at him, sat up, and undid the contraption herself. He fell greedily upon her breasts.

When he tired of them, he set to her pants. She raised her hips from the couch, allowing him to pull them free. She reached back and pushed the swing again. Her nephew gurgled and swatted at the rattle mounted before him. The boy finally realized that the swing mechanism was broken.

They were both down to underwear and he ground himself into her. It wasn't a particularly good feeling—something like the early stages of rug burn—but he couldn't bring himself to stop. When he came poking out the front of his boxers, he didn't reach to return it—the grinding felt much better against the satin of her underwear than it did against the cotton of his own.

"You want to?" he said.

Colleen shook her head.

He paused. "You sure?"

She nodded.

He had raised himself up off her to speak. Doing so exposed her breasts, and he fell upon them again with his hands and mouth, as if he had forgotten they existed. He kept up the grinding of pelvises and soon he found himself pulling her underwear aside. His aim always seemed skewed. He finally used a hand for direction, but as he slid his hips forward, Colleen stopped him.

"No," she said. She looked over her shoulder toward her nephew.

He pushed his hips farther forward, stopping only when their hips met. They remained motionless for a moment, staring into each other's eyes. She weakly shook her head. He nodded.

"At least put something on," she said.

He sat up and reached down for his pants, scuffling about for his wallet. When he set to putting the rubber on, it proved difficult, impossible, really.

"You've got it backward," she said.

He corrected his mistake and fell back upon her after he finished with the condom. She kept one hand on the swing, rocking it steadily. There was again the question of aim, but with some help from his hand, he corrected it. As he proceeded through the motions, he heard noises from Colleen. He wanted to believe that the sounds were evidence of pleasure, evidence that he was doing something right. As he continued, he realized she was humming. By the time he'd finished, he could tell that the tune was something of a lullaby, and not meant for him at all.

He sat up and stared at the television. There was a movie on. He tried to catch up with what he had missed. Colleen stood up quickly and grabbed her clothes. Before she left the room she glared back at him and said, "Are you happy?" She looked angry. "Now that you can tell your friends?"

He thought it strange. He didn't have friends. And if he told the friends he once had, they would most certainly kick his ass. And she knew this. When she came back into the room, she was clothed. She took her nephew and left again. The boy put his pants back on. She returned without the child and took a seat in a chair across the room from him.

"That was my first time," he said.

"What?"

"I've never done it," he said. He thought it was obvious.

She came slowly toward him. She took up a seat on the couch. "Really?"

"Yeah," he said. He grabbed his T-shirt off the floor. He turned it right side out and reached his hands above his head to pull it on.

"What are those?" Colleen said, touching the inside of his arm.

He flinched and quickly pulled the shirt down and over his head. He looked at the television and tried to let the moment pass.

"Hey," she said. She tried to lift his elbow, but he held his arm tightly to his side. "What happened?"

"It's nothing," he told her.

"It's not nothing," Colleen said.

"It's old," he said.

Colleen shook her head. "One's still scabbed."

He stared at the television.

"Hey," she said. She tugged at his hand.

He looked at her. He shook his head.

They both looked back to the television.

"When I was in middle school," Colleen said. "I rubbed a pencil eraser back and forth on my arm. I made a cross. The counselor kept saying it was because of my parents' divorce, but I was just bored."

"It's not like that," he said.

"Don't get mad," she said. She put her head on his shoulder and wrapped her arms around him. She held him quietly for some time. "Have you told anyone about Bobby?" she said.

"My mother."

"Any of your friends?"

He shook his head.

"Will you tell me now? What happened?"

"He died," the boy told her.

"What was it like?"

He thought for a moment. "Not wicked bloody or anything like that," he said. "He just stopped."

"Stopped what?" Colleen said.

"Stopped everything."

A commercial break came on the television and he slipped out of her embrace. He eased her down on the couch and slid his hand up under her shirt. He ran the tip of his index finger around her nipple. He pulled her shirt up and sucked at her breast. His pelvis started to gyrate against the outside of her thigh.

"Already?" she said.

He looked up and smiled.

After it was over, Colleen smiled and said, "You're not lying? I'm your first?"

He nodded. "You?" he said.

"Once before," she told him. "Twice now."

He raised his eyebrows at what he thought was a lie.

"I thought I was in love with him," she said.

"Punk-rock guy?"

"Yeah," she said. "How did you know?"

"Youth guys," he said.

"What else did they tell you?"

He shook his head.

"You shouldn't believe them," she said. "They know I don't believe in any of their shit."

He nodded. They put on their pants and watched what was left of the movie.

Jenny and Doug came back squinting and yawning. They said thank you and good-bye. Colleen and the boy walked through the drizzle to the car, and after they were back on the highway, he said, "You won't tell?"

"About the drinking?" she said.

"And us?"

Colleen paused for a moment. "No," she said.

It made the boy half happy. Half happy because it was one of the two things he had been fretting about. He was also concerned about returning to his house half drunk and late. It was Friday. He knew his father was due home and hoped he would be sleeping. If all went well, he could slip quietly into his room, tell his parents a half-truth the following morning, and everything would turn out half good.

They were about two hundred feet from his driveway when he said, "Stop here."

"What?" said Colleen.

"Stop," he said. "Stop, here."

"They know you're with me, right?"

"Don't pull in," he said. "Keep going, keep going." He grabbed the steering wheel and pulled the car back onto the road.

"Why?"

"Pull over up there, past the house," he said. Colleen coasted the car to the spot he directed her to. She stopped the car, but kept it running. She looked straight ahead.

"What?" he said.

She shook her head.

"Come on," he said. "I'm already late."

"Did you even say you were with me?"

"Yes."

"Then why don't you want me to drop you off?"

"It's not that," he said. "My dad's home. I don't want to wake him up."

"I thought your parents were divorced."

"I never said that."

"He's never here," she said. "I just thought—"

"He moved for work. My mom and I will too."

"Move?" she said. "When?"

"When the house sells."

"Why didn't you say?"

He shrugged.

She looked out the window.

"I'm late," he said. "I got to go."

The two leaned in and exchanged a quick peck. He left the car and tried to close the door as quietly as possible.

At the front porch he took his shoes off, to creep more quietly. The decking was wet but the porch was creaky as hell. He inserted the key and slowly turned the bolt. Once the door was free of the jamb, he swung it quickly to avoid the haunted-house groan that happened if it opened slowly. He held his breath to hear. The furnace kicked on with a rumble. He stepped inside and set his loafers down.

As he made his way to the kitchen, he saw his father's slippered feet propped up on the coffee table in the living room. He stopped. He could see the hem of his father's blue bathrobe.

"What are you doing up?" he said. The stairway blocked any eye contact between the two.

"Can't sleep," the father said, in the hushed tone of a man with a wife asleep in the house. The boy walked around the front of the stairs and entered his line of sight. The father looked up over a paperback, the title declared in a daunting raised font on the front cover.

"A little late?" he said, looking back to his book.

The boy shrugged.

"What you been up to?"

"Hanging out."

"She says you got a girl. The ex of one of these political guys."

The boy nodded.

"You be careful."

"They were broke up," he said.

"You watch out for her too," the father said. "Don't go and get yourself hurt."

The boy nodded.

"Still no word on the charges," the father said.

He shook his head.

The father nodded. "I'd be calling it a night. We got a funeral in the morning."

"Who?" the boy said.

"Lawrence," the father said. "Your mother's uncle."

"How?" the boy said.

"Diabetes, mostly. Then he killed himself. Apparently."

"How?"

The father made the shape of a gun with his hand and put his index finger in his mouth. The cocked hammer of his thumb fell.

"Wow," the boy said.

The father reached for the fallen book with his open hand. The boy stooped and handed it to him. "Sleep tight," his father said.

The boy stood for a moment before he nodded and left.

In the darkness of his room he pulled the covers over his head, and in the confines of his sheets his body convulsed in several quick sobs. He didn't tell his father that he loved him, or that he was glad to see him. And he did. And he was. Something had grown up between the two.

When the boy's childhood dog had been struck down in the street, there had been such a draw to his father, that, once in his arms, the boy stayed there for hours. He buried his face in his father and hid there, crying and soaking his shirt. His father rubbed warm circles across his back.

But now it was as if the poles had reversed. The closer the boy and father became, the harder they pushed each other away. The boy felt broken up and confused. There was something that he couldn't get his head around. He wished he could still seek comfort in the father's arms, but his body chose instead to turn in on itself, milking the last warm remnants of the night's beer buzz.

He ran his fingers over the scars and scabs on the inside of his arm. Each was in the shape of a simple smiling face. The rollers of the lighter formed two eyes, the curved metal flame guard a deep smile. When the boy made a muscle in the bathroom mirror, they all stared back at him, laughing.

13

It was a Catholic service and, like most, it did little for the boy. He was bored by all the repetition. And they were stuck with Father Thomas—he was in his seventies and his recent hip replacement had aged him considerably more. At one point in the service Father Thomas started saying *Clarence* instead of *Lawrence*. The boy scarcely knew his great-uncle, but from what he gathered, his life had grown difficult. The diabetes he'd managed for most of his life had finally overrun him. It had sapped a good deal of his sight and worked on his legs—subtracting from them a joint at a time—leaving him confined to a wheelchair, half blind.

He did it with a .45 pistol, in his mouth. They found him behind the barn, as he told them they would. He had said, "You
got yourself a lame horse, you know what you do: You take it
out back, you take care of it." The story of him saying this
went around and around at his service. Perhaps to help purge
the guilt of those who had actually heard him say it and had
done nothing, or maybe because some found it eerily noble, as
some final expression of virility. It seemed like strength, control, some manifest destiny. In the action, Lawrence had pro-
claimed: *I cannot live my life as I would like; therefore I
assume the responsibility of ending it.* Or perhaps it was more
like: *This sucks—fuck it.*

The ceremony at the cemetery had an altogether different effect on the boy. His great-uncle had served in Korea and he
was buried with full military honors. The boy had never seen
anything like it. He watched the soldiers in full dress march
through the procedure. There were two things that broke him
up: The first—while folding up the flag from his great-uncle's
coffin, one of the soldiers was clearly in tears. The image of
that sadness amid the formality was wrenching. The boy
thought he must have been a relation, but at the end, he left in
the ROTC van without a word to anyone. The second thing
was the gunfire. The first shots were so sharp and so startling
that the boy flinched, and in this motion something seemed to
come loose in him. The man calling out the command for the
shots had a southern accent and it came out, *Aiem, faher!* As
the shots continued, they grew less shocking, but for some reason he didn't want them to end. *Aiem, faher!* There was something tremendously beautiful about it. *Aiem, faher!* By the last

volley the boy was choked up and wet in the eyes. It confused
him. He'd never really known the guy.

After the services there was a get-together at the local Elks'
Lodge. The family had congregated there time and again for
wedding and funeral receptions, graduation parties and wedding anniversaries. It was an enormous sharp-white Victorian
building of three floors. From the windows at the front there
was a beautiful view of the lake. During the many events in the
past the boy and several cousins had explored what they could
of the building. In the basement they'd found a bar at the head
of six bowling lanes. The boy was the first to get a running
start and baseball-slide into the pins. On the third floor the
kids thought they had found an illegal gambling operation
when they discovered a room with a roulette wheel, tables for
craps, poker, and blackjack. The father, hearing of the conspir-
acy, chuckled and said, "It's pretend—they use play money,
for charity." And then more seriously, "The hell you doing up
there? Stay where you belong."

The father, the mother, and the boy stood in the middle of
the room that ran adjacent to the first-floor bar and looked
out upon the lake.

"Donna?" the father said. "Whiskey and ginger?" The
mother nodded. The grandfather and grandmother left another circle of folks and approached them.

"You all set?" the father said to his in-laws. He made a motion to the bar. The two held up their usual cocktails—the
grandmother a Manhattan, the grandfather scotch and water.

"Come give me a hand," the father said. The boy followed.
The father rested on the bar, a twenty in his hand so that

the bartender would know his intentions. It was only slightly past noon and it was a funeral reception, but still the bartender was rushed. It was this way with the family. The father made a motion for the boy to stand next to him at the bar.

"I been thinking," he said to the boy. "Seems like you've been having a hard go of it."

The boy nodded. His father handed him his mother's cocktail and grabbed his own after carrying out the transaction with the bartender.

"You want," said the father, "you can come down and stay with me."

The boy nodded. "Yeah," he said.

"That's it?" said the father. "'Yeah'?"

The boy shrugged.

The father shook his head and turned away. The boy stood for a moment and watched his father walk back to the family. He looked across the room and saw the lake through the wall of windows. He didn't know why, but he didn't want to go to Pennsylvania with his father.

The boy's mother was busy talking to his grandparents when he approached, so he waited at her elbow until there was a break in the conversation. He handed her the drink.

"Well, Teddy." His grandmother pulled him by the back of the neck to kiss his cheek.

"Hey, Grandma," the boy said.

His grandfather reached out his hand and the boy shook it. He was an old man, but his hand was still heavy and hard. He had broad forearms and his neck was thick like a linebacker's.

"Howdy, Chief," his grandfather said.

"Grandpa," the boy said. He nodded and stayed silent so as

to allow their conversation to resume. In no time they were talking about Lawrence. They agreed that it was a shame, but his grandmother claimed that if he'd taken better care of himself he would've lasted longer. She said that a diabetic shouldn't have drunk like he did. When the boy felt that they had sufficiently forgotten his presence in their conversation, he left the circle.

He went to a corner and stood alone, watching other groups about the room. He felt uneasy in large gatherings of his family. They were strangers, after all, for the most part. Sure, they were allowed to hug and kiss you, but this made it worse. Most of them only saw one another on these ceremonial occasions—and that didn't seem to constitute an intimate relationship. Yet somehow it did. He looked for his uncle John, but he was nowhere to be found. John had arrived late to the funeral and remained standing at the rear of the church. At the burial he stayed out along the fringes of the crowd.

The boy crossed the room to the buffet on the far wall. Passing over the two tin pans of lasagna, he noticed that his grandfather was choosing from the several bowls of coleslaw. Before leaving the line, the boy split a dinner roll and stuffed it with roast beef from the cold-cut plate at the end of the table. He found a small bowl of shock-yellow mustard and doused the makeshift sandwich.

He chose a folding seat at a round folding table that was covered with a linen cloth. He was surprised when his grandfather took a seat just two chairs over. As a child the boy had felt a distinct dislike from his grandfather, but as he had grown he'd realized that the grandfather seemed annoyed by all children. They frustrated him with their dependence and their inadequacy.

"Say I shouldn't eat like I do," his grandfather said. "Say I'll end up like old Lawrence there. Well, not like him, I suppose."

"He was your younger brother?" the boy asked.

"Yup, old Lawrence," said the grandfather. "Weren't like brothers you'd think today. They didn't let kids stay 'round much."

The boy nodded.

"How's it sit with you?" the grandfather asked him. "The way he done it?"

The boy didn't know what answer his grandfather was looking for, so he used a mouthful of sandwich as an excuse to shrug.

"Women seem upset," the grandfather said. "Don't bother me none." The grandfather ate a forkful of coleslaw. "I take a man's word. You?"

The boy nodded.

"Some ways are just no way. You follow me?"

The boy nodded again.

"Weren't like that boy that got himself killed," the grandfather said. "What was his name?"

"Bobby," said the boy. "Bobby Dennison."

"Now that's a goddamn shame. At his age?"

The boy nodded.

"They still investigating?"

The boy's mouth was full with a bite of sandwich, so he didn't respond.

"Doesn't seem right, really. You didn't do nothing wrong," the grandfather said. "Leaving a couple fools with a gun ain't

the brightest thing I ever heard, but how can you be held responsible for something they did on their own?"

"I don't know," the boy said.

"What you think will come of it?"

The boy shrugged.

The two ate in silence for some time.

"Old Lawrence," the grandfather said. "Now there was
one miserable son of a bitch. Told me once, 'I wouldn't piss on
you if you were on fire.'" He raised an eyebrow and nodded
at the boy. "Just the way he was. Probably ain't right to talk
like that but he was never one to try to tell you what a sweet-
heart he was."

After saying their good-byes, the father, son, and mother
walked across the parking lot. The mother put her arm
through the boy's and squeezed it tight.

"What'd you and your grandfather talk about?"

"Suicide."

"What'd he say?"

"Thinks it's fine," he said.

"I don't know what makes them think they have the right,"
she said.

"They're a different generation," the father said. He unlocked the car doors and they climbed in.

"Doesn't matter," she said. "You can't do that to your family."

"I'm sure he thought he was doing them a favor," the father said.

"If he even thought about them at all."

"I'm just saying he probably felt like he was a burden."

"It's selfish," she said.

"Can we talk about something else?" the father said. "Something decent?"

"Yes," said the mother. "You're right."

"Thank you."

A moment of silence passed before the boy blurted out, "I don't want to move to Pennsylvania."

"Did you hear your father?" the mother said. "He drove eight hours to spend the weekend with us—the least we can do is make it time well spent. Right?"

The boy remained silent.

"Well?" the mother asked again.

"This is fucked," he whispered.

"What?" she said.

"Nothing," said the boy.

"What did you say?"

"We're so screwed up."

The mother spun in her seat and shot a finger in the boy's face. "Don't you ever say that about my family. You don't have the right. Did you ever stop to think why we're in this mess?"

"Back off," the father hollered. "The both of you."

The mother turned and sat back in her seat. The car was silent until the boy heard the mother's pained and sporadic breathing.

"We're fine," she sobbed. "Everything is fine." Her voice was hollow and aching. "It's just the funeral," she said. "Everyone's a little emotional, that's all. A little overtired—we just need some rest. Everything's fine," she repeated. "We're fine."

The boy wanted to open the door and jump from the moving vehicle, haul ass into the woods, and hide there. Instead, he found himself pondering Lawrence's suicide. He tried to imagine what he might do in the position of Lawrence's children—if it had been his father to put the gun in his mouth and pull the trigger. What would he do with the pistol that had taken his father's life? Of course he would have to wait for the police to finish their investigation and rule out wrongdoing before he could even have access to it, but after that, what?

The boy imagined retrieving it—bagged as it had been found—and some night, after his mother had gone to sleep, he would take it to the kitchen sink and wash the sidearm free of his father's remains. Covering the kitchen table with newspaper, he would disassemble the gun and clean its intricacies to the best of his ability. Oiling the many moving parts, he would put it back together and wrap the gun in the light-blue felt of a Crown Royal bag. Then what? Sell it? The thought sickened him. Bury it? It seemed such a waste.

The boy leaned his face against the cool glass of the window and watched the passing world. They were nearly home and the car was quiet. He turned away from the window, where everything was dark and indistinguishable, and looked at the shadowed dome of his father's head. He was happy it was whole. He was glad he didn't have to see inside.

14

I n school the following Monday, Colleen held the boy's hand in front of people. She held her head up to be kissed when they parted, even when the hallway was busy with other students. The boy did his best at making minor, casual objections, but he finally blurted out, "We can't do this."

"Why?"

"*Why?*" he said.

"We're together."

"I'm going to get my ass kicked."

"You're afraid of them," she said.

"Shut up." He stormed down the hallway to his next class.

Later in the day Colleen approached him at his locker. She tugged on his shirt.

"I'll talk to George," she said. "I'll make him understand."

"Are you kidding?"

"Teddy."

"That's retarded," he told her.

"Why are you doing this?"

He didn't respond.

"Hey." She tugged at the hem of his shirt again.

Still he didn't respond.

"You know what," she said. "You can fuck off."

He looked away from her.

"Fuck you," she said, and walked down the hall.

He didn't try to stop her.

He knew he wasn't handling it right. He couldn't understand it. Sex, intercourse—he had ached for it. At times he'd felt as though some vital inner organ would rupture if he remained without it any longer. But now he felt something else, and he didn't know exactly what or why. He thought he must be an idiot, maybe even gay, for here was Colleen—cute and nice and affectionate Colleen—and he couldn't even kiss her without wincing.

The kid and the couch and the broken swing—he wanted to forget it, and that was all the easier when she wasn't around.

When he walked into school the next day, the first Youth member he saw had a vicious sneer upon his face. A moment later, farther down the hall, two more members confronted him.

"You're so dead," Birch told him.

"After school, motherfucker, wicked dead," said a kid whose name he always forgot.

He and Peckerhead Jackson were lab partners in biology, and for the first half of the period Peckerhead managed to remain silent, but he was a talker and it was killing him.

Without looking up from his lab report, Peckerhead finally whispered, "What the heck, Ted?"

"What?" the boy said.

Peckerhead didn't reply.

"What, Peckerhead?"

When he finally said what was going around, the boy felt gut-shot. Point blank. The word passing through him, the concussion sending waves out from its place of impact somewhere in his torso. *Rape*. He felt himself sway. He wished his body would collapse. He wished he would fall and hit his head on something, lose consciousness, and wake up at home or in the hospital, anywhere other than third-period biology.

Peckerhead told him that Colleen had confessed the details of her night with the boy to Becky Stanton, another Youth member's girlfriend. Becky relayed the story to her own boyfriend and by the time it all got back to George Haney, it went like this: Ted LeClare got drunk and raped Colleen Crenshaw.

"She said she told you no," Peckerhead said.

"It wasn't like that."

"Did she say it?"

"It wasn't like that," the boy said.

"Did she say no, Ted?"

"I need to talk to them."

"They won't believe you," Peckerhead said.

"Because they want to kick my ass."

"No," Peckerhead said. "Because they want you back. If they can't have that, then they'll kick your ass."

"No way," the boy said.

Peckerhead shrugged. "Go up to George after school and tell him how sorry you are and see," he said. "You're his golden boy."

"Jesus," said the boy. "Why did you get me involved with them?"

"Because if I didn't, they could do this to me," Peckerhead said.

The boy shook his head.

He didn't follow his regular path to his next class. He walked straight to where he thought he'd find the only person who might help him—his childhood friend, and known bruiser, Terry Duvall. Terry wasn't in the bathroom in the vocational wing, where he was known to smoke between classes, but on his way back, the boy found him sitting on a railing outside the building. The boy explained his predicament.

"Fucking slut," Terry said.

"What should I do?"

"They're pussies and shit-talkers," Terry told him. "You can get on my bus after school if you want."

"Thanks," the boy said.

"What were you doing with those cocksuckers anyway?" Terry said.

"I don't know."

"You find me," Terry told him. "I ain't going to go looking for you."

The boy nodded.

He skulked from class to class, staying away from his standard route. Whenever he saw a Youth member, he did what he could to avoid him, even if that required stopping and walking in the opposite direction. He was late to his last two classes because of the tangents he took.

While the last bell meant an end to this miserable day, the boy also knew it marked an open season on himself. Once off school property, he was fair game. He searched the herd of students making their way to the buses. When he saw Terry's orange hair, he struggled through the crowd to get to him.

Chris Awdry walked with Terry. While Terry had come to be a known bruiser, Chris was a known psycho. He was not right. The boy knew this. It was not an act with Chris Awdry. Chris scared the boy. This was the kid whose left nipple had been disfigured by a knife his sister threw at him when he was eleven. This was the kid who had set a bonfire in his own attic.

They made their way to the bus without trouble and took the seats at the back. The boy felt relieved when the door squealed closed and the bus groaned forward.

A couple of miles from school Terry said, "There they are."

On the road behind them was Jason Becker's Volkswagen Rabbit. At first the Rabbit was two cars back, but soon it rode close to the bumper of the bus. The car was packed full with Youth. They made every kind of violent and vulgar gesture known in the vocabulary of hands.

"Should we tell the driver?" the boy asked.

Chris didn't acknowledge the comment.

Terry just looked at him and smiled. "That's how they would do it," he said. "Ain't it?"

While the boy sat shifting uneasily in the green vinyl seat, Terry and Chris prepared themselves. Terry tied tight the work boots he normally wore loose and open. Chris took off his jean jacket and stuffed it in the boy's backpack. Then he jumped into a crouch between the last two seats and threw two middle fingers at the car behind them.

"Get in your seat!" the bus driver shouted from the front. Chris lingered a moment before heeding the command.

"There's a lot of them," the boy said.

"There's three of us," Terry said.

Chris looked at the boy and said, "Get a rock or a stick if you can."

Terry leaned over and looked out the back again, "When they ratted out Devo for dealing, some of that weed he had was mine."

When they got off the bus, Jason Becker stood with one foot out of his car, one hand on the roof and the other on top of the open door.

"This has nothing to do with you, Terry," he said.

The boy realized that it was true—this had nothing to do with Terry or Chris, and yet here they were, more inclined to go through with this fight than the boy was himself.

"Fuck you, peckerwood," Chris shouted.

"What do you know about it?" Terry said.

Becker's car was holding up traffic. He tried to wave the cars by, but they wouldn't pull around on the blind corner. When the car behind him began honking, Becker finally got in and pulled away in search of a more suitable pull-off or turn-around. As they passed, the Youth in the car were screaming through the windows, holding up middle fingers and fists. Terry and Chris stood their ground. The boy remembered how those same hands had shaken his own and patted his back. He had seen those screaming, bitter faces smile, warm with affection.

"Come on," Terry said to the boy, once the car had passed around a corner, out of sight. When the boy hesitated, Terry said, "Hurry up dumb-ass or they'll see us." Chris and Terry crossed the ditch on the far side of the road.

They picked their way through the woods, eventually coming out in Chris's backyard. There was an empty above-ground pool and a deck that ran between the pool and a sliding glass door on the house. Chris took a key from his pocket and unlocked the back door. He flipped open a pizza box that sat on the kitchen table and took a slice. He motioned for Terry and the boy to do likewise. They took the last three pieces—they were dry and curled at the edges, the cheese white and the crust difficult to chew.

Back out on the porch they smoked some pot from a small metal pipe. The smoke scorched the boy's lungs. Terry and Chris laughed as he coughed and hacked. Chris rapped the ash out of the pipe. "You guys hungry?" he said.

Terry and the boy shrugged.

"I'm starving," Chris said. "Got any money?"

He collected several dollars each from Terry and the boy. He pulled another couple of singles from his pocket. He walked inside to the foot of the stairs. "Hey, you want dinner?" he shouted.

"Here," a voice hollered down. Chris ran upstairs and returned with a ten-dollar bill. A moment later he was on the phone ordering two large cheese pizzas.

The boy felt safe at Chris's house. He doubted that any of

the Youth knew where Chris lived and he doubted even more that they would make any attempt to get at him there. Chris's fight with a senior the previous year was a part of the school's collective memory. There had only been about two dozen people present at the bout, but anyone could tell you what had happened. They said that Chris was half the senior's size. They said the senior asked for it, taunting Chris that way. They said that when it was over, the senior was not only missing his shirt but a front tooth and a good fistful of hair as well.

The three boys watched a movie on a pay station. The boy's body felt heavy and his mind slow, so slow. He felt like he was melting into the couch. He found himself stopping to remind himself exactly what was happening: *This is a movie, this is Chris's house, it is after school.* He dreaded the thought of ever having to leave—having to go home to his mother, stoned—having to leave the safety of Chris and Terry.

The boy jumped at the sound of the doorbell. Terry pointed at him and laughed. Chris got up and went to the door. When he returned, he put the two pizza boxes on the coffee table in front of them. He yelled at the ceiling, "Dinner! Hey!"

The boy leaned forward and took a paper plate and a slice of pizza. Behind him he heard someone descending the stairs. She had pajama bottoms on and a large T-shirt that hung nearly to her knees.

"You know Ted?" Chris said to her. She didn't look at the boy but she shook her head. "My sister, Shelly," Chris said to the boy.

"Hi," the boy said.

Shelly didn't respond. She took two slices of pizza and went back upstairs.

"She's just like that," Terry told the boy.

The boy had noticed that her nipples had protruded through her T-shirt. And the thought of her nipples led to thoughts of sex, which led the boy to thoughts of Colleen and the whole mess he was in. He did his best to think of something else. The pizza helped.

He waited until well after dark to leave and cautiously walked the side of the road, ducking into the woods when headlights appeared. The pot hadn't relaxed him. He heard cars approaching that were not cars approaching but wind in the woods. When he ducked off the road, he went much farther than was necessary. He found himself walking deeper still into the forest, even after the car had come and gone. He had to remind himself: *I'm walking home; home is that way.*

He walked in the front door and kicked off his shoes. The house was warm and smelled of food. He heard the television.

"You with the boys?" his mother asked.

He hung up his jacket and dropped his backpack at the foot of the stairs. "Nah," he said.

"No?"

"Remember Terry?" he said.

"Duvall?" she said. "Of course. Is he friends with the boys now?"

"No," he said. He walked into the living room. He did his very best impersonation of a sober boy.

She had her legs pulled up on the couch and an afghan draped over them. A dirty plate and fork sat on the coffee table in front of her. The television was on. He smiled quickly

at her and passed through to the kitchen. A casserole dish of
chicken breasts cooked in cream-of-mushroom soup rested on
the stove. A pot of rice pilaf sat next to it. He took a plate and
a chicken breast, a scoop of rice. He ladled the sauce from the
casserole dish over both.

"You okay?" she asked him.

"Yeah," he said.

"You sure?"

He shrugged.

"Something with the boys?"

He shrugged again.

The mother stayed silent.

"They don't like me anymore."

"No?"

"Nope." He was eager for the chicken and rice, despite the
three slices of pizza at Chris's house.

"Was it Colleen?" the mother asked.

He shrugged.

"You know, I thought she was trouble," the mother said. "I
should've done something."

He nodded. He ate quickly and rinsed the plate before putting it in the dishwasher.

"I'm going upstairs," he told her. "Do some homework."

"Okay," she said.

In his room he fell into a panic. He had seen the commercials, "No means no." And Colleen had said no. But it hadn't
been like that. Or had it? By law he was guilty, wasn't he? Yes,
but it hadn't been like that. It hadn't been. They'd had sex
after that. After that she'd said yes. How did she explain that
to George? How did they explain that?

The lethargy he'd experienced earlier had transformed into a terrible paranoia. He wasn't getting anywhere and he wished for some way to extract the marijuana chemistry from his mind, some antidote to slow down the ideas and quell the whirlwind in his head. For several hours he sat on his bed with his history book open, and in that time he never finished reading the section he'd started on. Finally there was a knock on his door.

"You still awake?" his mother asked.

"Yeah," he said.

She let herself in.

"I'm reading," he said.

"Any good?" She looked at the book splayed before him.

He shrugged.

"Sure that's the only thing keeping you up?"

"Yeah, Ma. I have to do it."

"You don't want to talk?"

"I'm fine, Ma. Just stop. Please."

"You haven't told anyone, have you?" she said.

He shook his head.

"What happened with Kevin and Bobby? Not even Colleen?"

"No, Ma. Jesus."

"You can't trust anyone," she said. "See how quickly they can turn on you?"

He nodded. "I know."

She bent over and hugged him. "Good night," she said.

"Good night."

He remained rigid against her embrace. Rather than look at his mother, he kept his eyes on the text that explained some event a hundred years prior. When she left, he gave up on the book and threw it to the floor. He pushed himself up and sat on the edge of the bed, both his elbows resting on his knees. He pushed up his sleeve on the left side. The inside of his upper arm was growing cluttered with the small, smiling burns. It hurt, somewhere inside, to see his body so abused. But there was something else in him that said he deserved it, that told him he deserved worse—it wanted to cover his whole body with the burns, it wanted worse. He winced and shook his head, but it wouldn't stop.

He held the lighter out and flicked the flame to life. He counted slowly. He moved his thumb back from the rollers, maintaining pressure on the plastic tab, keeping the flame alive. When he passed one hundred, he turned the lighter around in his hand and gripped it. He rested his opposite arm across his thigh, his palm facing the ceiling. He brought the hot metal down on the inside of his forearm. His arm bucked to get away, but he held it there as the heat of the metal dissipated into his flesh. He leaned back on his bed and let the lighter fall away.

His mind was clear for a moment, but soon the same circle of thoughts plagued him again. No matter how he went about it, he always came back to the fact that she had shaken her head. It hadn't been like that, he told himself. But it had. But it hadn't. But it had.

15

For the rest of the week, the boy took Terry's bus and waited at his house for a couple of hours before heading home. To be safe, he walked in the woods and along an old railroad grade that paralleled one of the roads between their homes.

He was quickly developing a habit of smoking grass. Terry handed him small amounts in the twisted-off corners of sandwich bags and in turn the boy gave him a five- or ten-dollar bill. If it was early he went for a walk in the woods, and if it was late he turned off his bedroom lights, stuffed pillows under the covers, and proceeded out the window to the roof.

There were times that were quite beautiful: stars, the smells of wood—living, dying, and dead—the silhouettes of large pine boughs rocking in the wind. There were also times when he panicked over a sound in the house and everything went to shit.

While most of what had occurred in his life could account for his general ill feeling, it was another run-in with the Youth that had made one of the days notably worse than the rest.

He'd come face-to-face with Colleen in the school hallway between periods. There was a moment where neither of them spoke.

"I didn't say it like they said it," she said.

He nodded.

"I didn't," she said. "I swear."

"I figured."

"I'm sorry," she said.

"Me too."

"They can't stop talking about it." She pouted and he felt like he was falling for her all over again. "No matter what I say. It doesn't matter."

"I know what you mean," he said.

"I thought they'd be over it faster." Suddenly she looked over his shoulder. Her smile disappeared and she looked at the floor. Before the boy could look back, a hand grabbed his shoulder and spun him around.

"What are you thinking?" Jason Becker barked at him.

He froze, a frightened stare on his face.

"You think you can talk to her?" Becker said it loudly enough that the kids coursing down the hallway looked. Some even stopped to look.

The boy looked over his shoulder for Colleen, but she was gone.

"Don't think we've forgotten," Becker said, "you degenerate fuck." Becker reached up and put his hand on the boy's face. He gave him a hard shove and the boy stumbled backward, knocking into several people. The girl that took the brunt of it whined, "What the fuck?"

The boy turned and apologized.

"Asshole," she said.

When the boy looked back, Becker was leaving, but there was a crowd staring at him. When he walked away he heard someone say under his breath, "What a pussy."

The worst part was that he knew he was to blame for all of it. He couldn't complain. He couldn't bitch. But he could get stoned. Now he gave a quick glance in each direction of the railroad bed and pulled the joint out of his pocket. It was in an empty pack of gum for protection and it had a slight air of mint because of that. He stopped for a moment to get it lit, and once it was burning, he continued on.

He tried to imagine a train passing on this grade that once had held tracks. It seemed so hard to believe, a train where now there was only an overgrown path in the woods. There were elaborate stone bridges where the trail passed over creeks and culverts and there were other reminders around town of some other time. As kids they'd found stone walls in the woods that seemed absurdly obsolete—dividing only forest from forest.

On walks during hunting season, the grandfather had pointed out the ruins of the first Darling farmhouse. The stone foundation was six or seven feet deep, with small trees growing out of the basement floor. The boy and his friends had found their way back to it, daring one another into the small, dark root cellar. There was a narrow stone well that made them think of the stories of children falling into such small, tight places.

The grandfather had told him about his days working on the farm: hay season, jacking deer, the farmer beating him worse than his father ever could. It was the Depression and the great-grandparents sent the grandfather away. At the farm they could feed him, and the farmer occasionally brought food to his parents as payment for his labor.

The boy thought about his grandfather's situation and felt a flash of guilt—here he was, well fed and underworked, and still such a screwup. An ache grew in him, and he closed his eyes and crooked his neck to hit at the joint. He hardly coughed anymore, but he flinched when he looked up—Mr. Benson, in a headband and sweatsuit, jogged toward him on the path. He tried to let his arm fall casually to his side, and he flicked the joint over the edge of the trail. He turned his head to the side and let the smoke slowly out of his nose.

"Hello, Teddy," Mr. Benson said.

"Hey, Mr. Benson."

Mr. Benson kept jogging and disappeared as quickly and as quietly as he had come. "Fuck," the boy said under his breath. "Goddamn fuck-all."

He turned, and when he saw that Mr. Benson was long gone, he went back and retrieved the joint. He hit at it several more times, snuffed it out, and slid it back into the empty pack of gum.

"The luck I got," he said. He remembered the hot afternoons he and his father had spent fishing on Mr. Benson's boat. He wondered if Mr. Benson had recognized the smell of pot. Then he wondered if Mr. Benson would fink on him.

The boy arrived home to an empty house. He went first to the bathroom and brushed his teeth. Then he tipped his head back and held each eye open for a couple of drops of Visine. He wiped at the corners of his eyes with the sleeve of his shirt and left the bathroom. In the kitchen he filled a bowl with pretzels, pulled a pickle out of a jar in the fridge, grabbed one of his mother's diet sodas, and went to the living room to watch television. After several sit-com reruns, his mother arrived. She had stayed late at school for a PTA meeting and picked up a pizza on the way home. The two greeted each other and made their way to the kitchen to eat. The house was quiet without the television on.

"Did you talk to Mr. O'Rourke?" she said.

"Nah," he said, chewing on one of those little pieces of sausage that reminded him of rabbit turds.

"Theodore," she said.

"What?"

"He gave you a D on your last exam." She whispered it, like she didn't want anyone else in the empty house to hear about her son's grade.

"It's just French," he said. "What am I, going to France?"

She shook her head. "Should I tell your father?"

"He said pay attention to my *important* classes." He took a bite of the crust that lay on his plate. "I got B's in algebra and technology." He said it through his half-chewed pizza and his mother shook her head some more.

"B minuses do not count as B's."

"They're not C's, are they?" he said. "Then they must be B's. Ma—"

"Quit it," the mother said. "Nobody likes a wiseass." He

stopped. When she started cussing, he knew to listen. "The stove downstairs needs wood," she said. "I moved what was left upstairs before I left for school."

"Is there enough for tonight?" he asked.

His mother shook her head and he frowned. This meant he'd have to haul wood over the twenty-five yards that lay between their house and the woodshed. It wasn't a terrible chore, but he wondered why she couldn't have just left enough for the night. He also wondered why the hell they'd built the woodshed so far from the house in the first place. Or why they were so stingy that they couldn't let the oil furnace heat the place for a night.

The mother finished her usual two slices of pizza and conscientiously left two pieces for lunch the following day. She sat and watched her son devour his half of the pie. He stuffed down bite after bite and the orange grease of cheese and sausage collected at the corners of his mouth. He wiped his face with the back of his hand.

"Am I grossing you out?" he said.

"You need to eat if you want to grow," she said.

He shook his head. He wanted to disgust her.

"I want you to be big," she told him. "So when you get married and we dance, I can put my head right here," she patted the inside of her shoulder. "I want my hand to feel small in yours."

"That's gross," he said. He pushed his chair back and left the table.

As much as he resented having to get the wood, he couldn't deny that it was a beautiful night. The empty wheelbarrow bounced over the bumps and roots on the path to the wood-shed. The cool evening air felt good on his still half-stoned head. He looked up and saw a handful of stars through the thick pine boughs. He smelled the cut wood in the shed some ten or twenty yards before he got there. He remembered scampering to his father's lap in the evenings and the way he smelled after a day of cutting firewood—the thick scent of his perspiration mixed with chainsaw exhaust and the smell of the sawdust that still clung to his damp T-shirt. The father's fragrance often contained a hint of cheap American pilsner. A great fondness for the man welled up in the boy, but it was quickly followed by a tremendous ache—his father was so, so far from him, standing in the backyard as he was, half stoned and torn up as hell. He stood for a moment and waited for it to pass. When it wouldn't, he set to his work anyway, wiping at his nose with the coarse collar of his work glove.

He was back inside, unloading his third wheelbarrow of wood, when he heard his mother call down to him.

"What?" he shouted at the unfinished ceiling of the basement.

"Get up here," she hollered.

"Goddammit," the boy said to himself. He threw off the heavy leather gloves and set to shedding his boots for the trek upstairs.

When he turned the corner at the top of the stairs, he saw Officer Duncan standing with his mother by the front door. The boy's mind raced at the sight. He thought of the half-smoked joint in his bedroom. He thought of Mr. Benson and wondered if he'd finked on him.

"Evening, Teddy," Duncan said.

The boy nodded and stopped where he was, halfway down the hall.

"He wants to talk to you," the mother said.

"Come here—I ain't going to bite," Duncan told him.

The boy closed the distance between them and jammed his hands in his pants pockets.

"I want to start by saying this is an unofficial visit."

"What's that mean?" the mother asked him.

"Means no one sent me. Means I'm here on my own."

Neither the boy nor his mother responded.

"I'm here as a friend. To tell you I think they've got a case against Theodore." Duncan shifted his weight from one foot to the other. "I can't say specifics but . . . do you mind if I come in and have a seat and we can talk about this?"

"I think it's best if you stay where you are," the mother said.

Duncan nodded. "I think it would look good if Teddy came clean. He could say he was in shock and afraid and not think-ing right. I think we'd have a much better chance of getting him off."

"I think you should leave," the mother said.

"Donna? You've known me a long time, haven't you?"

"Yes I have," she said. "But I've also lived here all my life and I can see how things are." She shook her head and rubbed at the bridge of her nose. "You're going to scapegoat this kid so you all can come out looking shiny as hell and so you can keep selling off this town as a country club. You think they're going to start moving here again if one of these kids gets killed and no one gets punished for it? Damn right they're not. And more people eventually means more money for each of you, I know it. I know how it is, Dick."

Duncan stood speechless for a moment. "That's quite a scheme you got cooked up," he said. "But it ain't right. I'm trying to tell you the best way through this thing that I can see. I'm insulted. I've always been square with you two."

"Say what you want, Dick, but this is my boy." She pointed at him. "The only one I got in this world. Now, you want him, you can take him, but know that you're going to have come through me. Because without him, nothing in this world means a thing to me." She stopped and wiped at the outside corners of her eyes. "Now, *as a friend*," she said. "I'm going to have to ask you to leave, kindly."

"All right. But this is all I can do for you. This is the end of the road for me."

The mother nodded and closed the door behind him. She turned and looked at the boy. His eyes were wet. She stepped close and put her arms around him. He didn't take his hands out of his pockets, but he let his face fall to her shoulder. His torso jumped with quick sobs.

"Don't you think we should tell?" he said.

She shook her head. "They can lie, you know. They can say whatever they want to try and get you to talk. It's legal for them to do it. I bet you anything he's here because they hit a dead end. I bet they're saying the same thing to Kevin as we speak."

"You think?"

"Don't worry," she said. "Trust me." She stepped back from him. "Now go and finish the wood so you can get to sleep."

He nodded and headed back down to the basement.

———

The following morning the boy showered and dressed. When he got to the kitchen, he found his mother at the table with her head in her hands. When she lifted her head, she looked distraught.

"What?" he said.

She shook her head.

"Mom?"

"I don't know why someone would do this to us," she said. She pointed at the front of the house. He walked to a window.

There was a helix of tire tracks across the lawn—brown dirt billowed over the grass where the tires had slid and spun. The mailbox had been knocked over and dashed in with a large rock that still sat atop it. The driveway bore two broken flowerpots, their soil spread in halos around them.

"Son of a bitch," he said. He took a deep breath.

"Do you know anything about this?" The mother stood behind him. "Could it be Kevin?"

He shook his head. He felt ready to explode. Hadn't Becker seen Colleen, smiling and talking with him? Wasn't that enough?

He winced when he heard his mother calling in sick.

"Something just came over me," she said. "I feel terrible."

The boy took the bus and fumed through school. Youth members smiled and chuckled at him in the hallways. He wanted to make a move on them: sucker punch one in the throat, throw a brick through a windshield in the parking lot, lob a Molotov cocktail through the storefront of George's mother's shop.

He found Terry at lunch and told him what had happened and what he wanted to do.

"No way," Terry told him.

"What?" the boy said.

"We mess with them, they tell on us," Terry said. "They're tattletales. You know the type."

"Piss off," said the boy.

"You want to do something, go right ahead," Terry said. "Just don't count me in."

The boy left the lunch room. He couldn't take the glaring eyes of the Youth any longer. He went to the bathroom and sat in the stall. If he'd had a cigarette he would have smoked it. If he'd had a lighter he would have burned himself. Instead he sat with his head in his hands, his elbows on his knees. He clenched his eyes as tightly as he could, but several small tears managed to push their way through the corners. He cursed himself for being so soft.

He skulked through the rest of the school day and took his bus home. When he got off at his stop, he saw that the mail-box was gone and the driveway clear of debris. As he crossed the lawn, he stepped over the tire tracks. The billowed dirt had been raked flat and sprinkled with pale flecks of grass seed.

He entered the house and greeted his mother but the two spoke little. He poured himself a glass of water and went to the couch. He turned on the television and bounced through the channels.

The phone rang and his mother answered it. By the tone of her voice, he knew it was his father. She spoke with him for a moment and then held the receiver out to him.

"He wants to talk to you," she said.

He shook his head.

She nodded and shook the phone.

He stood and wiped his mouth with the sleeve of his shirt. He crossed the room and took the phone.

"Hey," he said.

"What is going on up there?" the father said.

"I don't know."

"I find it hard to believe you know nothing about this lawn business."

The boy didn't speak.

"You can lie to me all you want," said the father. "But you tell whoever did it, I ain't you. When I come home I'm not going to lie in bed, pretending to be asleep while some kids tear up my property."

"Dad," he said. "I don't know who did it. I swear I didn't even hear them."

"This really helps sell the house, you know," the father said. "Me and your mother are killing ourselves trying to keep this family together and you keep doing the opposite."

"Dad—"

"Ted, I know about the drugs," the father said. "I got a phone call. And I got a good feeling this is something to do with that."

The boy held his breath. He didn't speak.

"Don't you think you've put your mother through enough?" the father said. "Don't you think? You're going to quit that right now. And you're coming down here with me soon as we can do the paperwork for school. Understand?"

"What about Ma?"

"What part of this don't you understand?" the father said. "You're under investigation for manslaughter. You keep messing around and you're going to jail. Then what about your mother?"

"I don't want to go to jail." He choked it out and a silence came over the line. "Dad?" he said.

"Christ, Ted. I'll do everything in my power. Everything I can. But you got to quit doing this stuff that can get you there. Understand?"

"Yes," he said.

"Say it," the father said. "Tell me you understand."

"I understand."

"Good," the father told him. "We'll get this all taken care of."

There was a moment of silence on the line.

"I don't want to move down there," the boy said.

"You say it like you have a choice."

"I do," he said. "I do."

"You know what a fool you sound like?" the father said. "You don't understand—"

The boy pulled the phone away from his head and held it at arm's length. He listened to the hollow outline of his father's voice at that distance. He turned the phone over and gently put it back in the receiver.

"If he calls back," he told his mother, "I'm not talking to him."

Later that night the boy sat at the desk in his bedroom. He struggled with his homework, distracted as he was. He heard the phone ring through the closed door of his bedroom. The ringing stopped and he heard his mother call his name. He stood and went to the hall.

"I'm not talking to him," he said.

"It's Terry," his mother called out from her bedroom.

He rumbled down the stairs and picked up the phone in the kitchen. He waited for the click of his mother hanging up.

"What's up?" he said.

"What are you doing?" Terry asked him.

"Homework."

"Can you get out?"

"Why?"

"Can you?"

"After she goes to sleep," he said. "Why?"

"Be out in your driveway at eleven."

He heard the click of Terry hanging up and he dropped the receiver back in the cradle. He went back to his room and sat at his desk. He struggled with his homework for the next hour and a half.

At ten-thirty he stuffed pillows under the covers of his bed. He wrote a quick note to his mother:

Mom,

Don't worry. I couldn't sleep. I went for a walk. I'll be back soon. I'm sorry about everything.

Love,
Ted

He folded it and put it on the pillow, where she would easily find it, were she to turn on the lights. He pulled on a pair of jeans, grabbed a hooded sweatshirt from his closet, eased open the door of his room, and stepped out into the hallway. He listened. One cautious step at a time, he walked down the hall and down the stairs, stopping at the bottom to listen again. He went through the dark living room, carefully weaving around the coffee table and footstool. He turned and went down the stairs into the basement. At the bottom he listened, and when he heard nothing from the house above him, he walked quickly across the cement floor to the door outside. He eased it open and closed as quietly as possible and went around to the front of the house.

The night air was sharp. It cut at his bare skin and he pulled up the hood of his sweatshirt and slid his hands into the pocket at the front. Autumn was upon them and the crickets no longer sounded. The boy felt as though he could smell the fallen leaves melting back into the forest floor. That was the smell of fall to him, the smell of decay.

He sat on the short stone wall that ran halfway down the driveway. When his butt grew cold and stiff, he stood and walked back up the driveway and across the sidewalk at the front of the house. In the moonlight he could just make out the front yard. He could see the fresh soil of the tire tracks. The anger began to grow in him again.

He heard footsteps in the sand at the end of his driveway and he saw Terry's silhouette out there in the darkness. The boy made his way down the walk and out to meet him.

"Hey," the boy whispered.

Terry nodded. "Come on," he said, waving the boy to follow. Terry took a right turn at the street. The only sound was their feet scratching at the sand on the side of the road. They came upon a car parked in the ditch. When Terry opened the door, the interior light came on and the boy saw that it was

Terry's mother's Ford. He stood for a moment, knowing that Terry didn't have a license, knowing that no good could come of this.

The boy knew he could shake his head. He could turn and walk back to his house and return to his bedroom. He could sit alone on the side of his bed and he could do the things he did to himself there. He flinched and shook his head. When Terry reached over and unlocked the passenger side door, the boy pulled it open and stepped in.

"You ready?" Terry said.

The boy shrugged. He could smell booze on Terry's breath. "You been drinking?" he said.

"You think I'd lift my mom's car sober?" Terry reached under the seat and came out with a bottle of liquor. It was flat and slightly rounded so as to fit conveniently in a back pocket of a pair of pants or the inside pocket of a coat. Terry unscrewed the cap, took a sip, and handed it to the boy. "Whiskey," he said, his eyes closed and his face winced in a sort of pucker. The boy took the bottle and pulled hard on it. The whiskey was hot and smoky in his mouth. Even hotter in this throat. He coughed quickly and took another hard sip. "Hey, go easy," Terry said.

"I got to catch up," the boy said.

"Case you ain't realized, I got a few pounds on you," Terry said.

The boy smiled and drank again from the bottle.

"Hey man, I'm serious," Terry said. He twisted the whiskey from the boy's hand. "We got shit to do."

"What you got in mind?" the boy said. He coughed into his hand.

"We're going to get back at those cocksuckers."

"The Youth?"

"Your mom . . ." Terry said. He took a sip from the bottle and screwed the cap back on. "Remember those multiplication tests? The timed ones?"

The boy nodded.

"Man, I just could not do those things. I'd break my pencil in the middle of the test to get out of it, you know? Your mom kept me in at recess for extra help and I must've broken five pencils one time. So obvious—but your mom never said a word. She just smiled and told me it was okay and let me try again."

"Yeah?" said the boy. He almost laughed at the thought of it.

"I'll kill those motherfuckers." Terry pounded a fist on the steering wheel. "Messing with your house like that." He pulled out a pack of cigarettes and rolled down the window. He flipped open the top and pulled one out between his lips. He held the pack out to the boy and the boy took one. "Roll down your window," Terry told him. "I can't have this thing stinking to hell." The boy did as he was told and Terry lit both of their cigarettes. He started the car, turned on the lights, and pulled out onto the road.

The boy's head started to spin from the nicotine and his body grew warm with the flush of alcohol. It felt wonderful. And as soon as he felt it, he was afraid the feeling would leave him.

"Give me some more," he said. He held out his hand. Terry reached under the seat for the bottle and handed it over.

"Go easy," he said. "I'm serious. We got work to do."

"You got a plan?" The boy took a long gulp and hissed between his teeth. "Yow," he said. He shook his head back and forth, back and forth. A flash of nausea rolled through him and he thought he would cool it on the booze for a bit.

"Yes," Terry said. "I got a plan."

The car rolled and wound through the wooded country roads. The boy was impressed with Terry's driving, although once he did drop two tires in the rocky ditch and the car bumped and rumbled until he jerked it back to the pavement.

The boy knew it was dangerous, driving with a drunk. He'd seen the commercials. He'd been subject to the campaigns in school. But to care about your physical well-being, you have to care about your physical well-being. The boy's drunk mind fantasized about crashing full speed into one of the broad pines on the side of the road—his body flying into the dashboard, through the windshield, headlong into the trees and small saplings. Pain was what his body craved. It pleaded to be burned and scalded and dashed to pieces. It longed for relief.

They took the back way out of town toward the high school. The boy wondered what Terry had in mind, but he didn't ask. Terry stopped at the intersection on the bypass. He looked both ways several times. He cautiously throttled the car out onto the two-lane and gently brought the car up to speed. He looked back and forth between the road and the speedometer, carefully working the throttle to keep the car at a steady speed.

The wind boomed through the windows, setting everything loose to fluttering. The car rolled over the uneven road like a

ship on the water. Terry bent his neck and took another cigarette from the pack with his lips. He couldn't get his lighter to
work in the wind so he reached down and pressed the lighter
in the dash. When it popped out, he retrieved it and set his cigarette to smoldering.

The boy looked across the car at Terry, illuminated by the
odd glow from the dash. The lights from the passing cars and
street lamps came in and over them, providing quick flashes of
clarity. The boy stared at Terry's hand on the wheel, the cigarette sprouting from between his fingers. Terry's left hand took
hold of the bottom of the wheel as he brought the cigarette to
his mouth. The red tip went bright as he inhaled. His hand returned to the wheel and he blew the smoke in the direction of
the open window. His eyes squinted and his lips were tight as
he forced the smoke out of his lungs. Looking at Terry, the boy
felt warm with something.

"Thanks," he said.

"Huh?"

"Thank you," the boy said.

"For what?"

"For everything."

"Don't start that."

"I'm serious," the boy said.

"You're drunk is what you are."

The boy shook his head.

"Drunk or queer," Terry said. "Take your pick."

The boy smiled and looked back out the windshield at the
tunnel the headlights created before them.

They passed the Haneys' gun shop. They passed the school.
Terry finally slowed the car and turned into the parking lot of

Jason Becker's apartment complex. He drove out to the far corner, where Jason's car sat alone. Terry smiled at the boy. He turned the car around and pulled back onto the bypass. He took the next left turn and after a couple hundred yards, he pulled over. He pointed at the woods.

"His car is that way," Terry told him. He took out the bottle and took a long drink. He handed it to the boy. "Finish it," he said. The boy was already reeling, but he took the bottle and did as he was told. He hardly flinched at the burn.

They got out of the car and Terry went to the trunk. He twisted the key in the lock and it popped. Terry bent over and came out with a small backpack. He threw it over his shoulder and it rattled.

The boy put his hand on Terry's arm. "What's in there?" he said.

"I'm doing this," Terry said. "You can come or not."

"Not his apartment," said the boy.

"Are you crazy?" Terry said. "That little piece-of-shit car of his."

"I don't know," the boy said. His tongue was thick with the whiskey and his voice sounded funny to him.

"You can come or not," Terry said. "This ain't for you anyway. This is for your mom." He turned and headed into the woods. The boy stood for moment but he quickly set off after Terry. He didn't want to be alone.

He had trouble walking in the woods. He stumbled on downed limbs and bumped into trees. The whiskey was working hard on him. He followed the sound of Terry's footsteps and the red glow of his cigarette. He was glad to see the woods open into the field above Jason's apartment complex. Before he stepped into the clearing, a briar patch got hold of his pants and drove thorns into his legs. He winced and set to pulling them free from his clothing. As he pulled them from his pants, they took hold of the arms of his sweatshirt. His predicament was getting worse. He grew frustrated and stood, tearing his arms up and away from the briars. He got balanced and forced his way step after step out of the patch. The vines ripped and popped out of his clothing and clawed at his skin. He stepped out into the grass of the field and it felt good to be free. Terry was halfway across the opening and the boy jogged to catch up, rubbing at the burning in his thighs where the thorns had got to him.

He caught up with Terry at a hedge just above the parking lot. Jason's car sat in the lot some twenty-five yards away. Terry had the backpack down on the ground and he fished two glass bottles out of it. He went back for some socks at the bottom and quickly assembled the Molotov cocktails.

"Whose socks you use?" the boy said.

"My brother's," Terry said, smiling. "I took the newest, cleanest pair I could find."

The two giggled for a moment.

Terry pushed one of the bottles at the boy, but he didn't take it.

"Come on," Terry said. "It'll be faster if we do it at the same time."

Still he didn't take it.

"Think about it," Terry said. "All they've done to you?"

The boy reached out and took the bottle in his fist. "Light it," he said.

Terry thumbed the lighter and held the flame to the socks.

They both watched the flames climb the cotton. "Let's do it," Terry said. He smiled at the boy and ran around the corner of the hedge. The boy followed. Terry ran half the distance to the car and hurled the bottle, but the boy kept running. He watched Terry's bottle crash to the pavement just under the driver's-side door. The flames burst and waved up to the window. The boy was hardly fifteen feet from the car when he let his go. The bottle crashed into the rear bumper and set the hatchback on fire. He stood for a second, admiring his throw, and then turned and sprinted. Terry was already gone. When the boy neared the tree line, he heard Terry call his name. He followed Terry's voice and found him hunched over, his hands on his knees.

"Holy shit," Terry said. "I can't believe you hit it."

The boy turned and watched the car burn. Terry's was nearly out, but flames still throbbed across the back of the car. The boy held his breath, waiting for the whole vehicle to catch, waiting for some grand explosion or finale, but the gas gradually burned off, leaving only the smoldering edges of a few bumper stickers.

"That's it?" said the boy.

"That's it," Terry said.

"It's not enough."

"He'll get it."

"It's not enough," said the boy.

"It's enough for tonight," Terry said.

The boy shook his head. He wanted to run back down the hill and jump on Jason's hood. He wanted to kick his foot through the windshield and piss all over the interior.

Terry reached over and took him hard by the arm. He

looked and Terry shook his head. He motioned back to the car with his head. "Come on, man," Terry said. "We should git."

He nodded.

Back in the car, on the way home, he looked over at Terry.

"My dad knows I been smoking dope," he said.

"How?"

"Mr. Benson caught me on the railroad bed."

"You ain't told on me?"

The boy shook his head.

"You better not," Terry told him.

"I won't," he said.

"What did he say?"

"I got to move down there with him."

"You going to?"

"Why not?" the boy said.

"Friends, I don't know."

"What friends I got?"

"You got me," Terry said.

"Yeah?"

Terry nodded. "You always had me."

The boy nodded. He set his jaw and tried to swallow the knot in his throat.

"Do I got you?" Terry said.

"Yeah," said the boy. "You do."

"Good," Terry told him.

16

The boy woke in desperate need to piss. He rolled over and stood, only to immediately take a seated position on the side of the bed. It felt as though someone had driven a nail behind his left eye. His stomach was acidic and pukey. His mouth tasted as he imagined the soles of his shoes might if he had walked through an ashtray and a puddle of vomit.

"Oh, good Christ," he hissed. He hung his head and clenched his eyes.

He took slow, cautious steps to the bathroom. Once there, he sat on the toilet to urinate, his elbows on his knees, his head in his hands. He stood and retrieved his underwear from around his ankles. He went to the sink and brushed his teeth.

He grabbed the bottle of mouthwash from below the counter and gargled to try to kill the whiskey he imagined was on his breath.

Back in the hallway, he leaned against the wall, looking down the stairs.

"Ma?" he hollered.

"Teddy?"

"Can you call in for me? I feel terrible."

"What's wrong?"

"I told you—I feel like crap."

"How so?" She came around the corner and looked up at him.

"I got a headache and I think I'm going to puke."

"Fever?" she said.

He shook his head.

"Come down and have something to eat," she said. "Maybe you'll feel better."

He shook his head. "I'm going back to bed. Just call in for me."

"Are you going to miss anything important?"

"Ma, come on."

"I think you should go."

"I think you should call."

She didn't say anything, just stared up at him.

"You owe me," he said.

"What?"

"Just do it, Ma."

"What do I owe you for, mister?"

He shook his head.

"Say it," she said.

"For keeping your secret."

She shook her head. "Ted," she said. She paused for a moment. "It's not my secret."

He leaned back and punched the wall. "Fine," he snapped. "Don't call in. I don't give a shit." He walked back into his room and slammed the door. He grabbed the chair from his desk and jammed it just under the knob. He tested the door and the chair held. He went to his bed and pulled the covers over him. He listened for his mother at the door, but the knob never moved. Sometime later he heard her car start in the drive and back out. After that he heard his bus come and go. He lay under the covers with his eyes clenched, but sleep would not come. The headache and the nausea and the fury kept him tossing.

Eventually he threw back the covers and got dressed. He went downstairs and poured himself a glass of water and fished a few aspirin from a bottle in the cabinet just beside the sink. He choked down the bitter, chalky tablets and went to the couch in the living room. He lay down and pulled the afghan from the back of the couch. He covered himself and reached out from under the blanket for the television remote. The tube sprang to life and he went through the channels until he found a station with morning cartoons. An episode of *Tom and Jerry* was in full swing. A clothes iron fell from its perch and struck the cat in the face. The cat's face took on the flat shape of the iron.

The boy was startled awake by a loud knock at the door. He sat up quickly and rubbed at his eyes. A commercial squawked from the television and the knock came again. He stood and looked out on the driveway. His body grew rigid at the sight of the local police cruiser. He crouched back down, out of sight of the windows. The knock came again, louder and more insistent. He knew it was Duncan. It had to be.

"Ted," a voice hollered from the other side of the door. It said something else but he couldn't make it out. He knew he could stay hidden. He knew he could lie on the floor and wait for Duncan to leave. But he also knew that doing so would only prolong whatever was coming.

He went to the door, turned the bolt, and drew it open. Duncan stood at the top of the stairs.

"Ted," Duncan said.

"Yeah?"

"You look tired."

"I was sleeping on the couch," he told him. "I'm sick."

"That's what they said at school."

He nodded, realizing that his mother had called in before she left. "My mom's not here."

"I know," Duncan said. "Feel like going for a ride?"

He shook his head. "Not really. I'm sick."

"Come on. Your parents wouldn't want people seeing the cruiser in the driveway." He pointed his thumb at the car.

"Since when do you care what my parents want?"

"Don't try to make me the bad guy, Ted," Duncan told him. "I've always been square with you."

He looked at the floor, embarrassed, because he knew Duncan was right.

"Get your shoes on. Come on."

He nodded and went to the living room to turn off the television. He took his keys from the kitchen table and walked back to the front door. He stepped into his shoes and grabbed his sweatshirt off the back of the chair beside the door. It had a slight smell of cigarette smoke.

They passed the entrance to Sandy Creek in silence. The boy eyed all the buttons and switches on the dash. The radio squawked now and again. When they neared Woodbury Heights, Duncan slowed the car and they turned in. He drove to the culvert at the top of the road and stopped. He put the car in park and looked over at the boy. The boy was afraid to turn his head.

"Hand me my lunch?" Duncan pointed to the brown bag near his feet.

He bent over and returned with the bag. He handed it over.

"I like to come up here to eat," Duncan said. "It's quiet, out of the way." Duncan opened the bag and rummaged around inside. He came out with a cellophane-wrapped sandwich.

"You like egg salad?"

The boy shrugged.

"Here," Duncan said, holding out half the sandwich. "My wife makes great egg salad."

"That's all right," said the boy.

"Take it." Duncan thrust the half-sandwich at him. "I've got a whole other one in here."

He took the sandwich and the two ate.

"It's good," the boy said, holding up the sandwich.

"Told you," Duncan said. "Chips?" He held out an open sandwich bag full of crinkle-cut potato chips.

The boy reached in and took one.

"Take a handful. You're doing me a favor. If I ate everything my wife packed, I'd be a blimp."

The boy reached over and took a few more chips. A little later Duncan offered him a cookie and he took it.

"You know why we're here?" Duncan said.

The boy shrugged. "Something with the Dennison case?"

"Yes and no." Duncan chewed and swallowed his last bite of cookie and chased it down with a sip from a can of diet cola. "They had a little incident over by the high school last night and I thought you might know something about it."

"What happened?"

"Someone tried to set a car on fire."

"Huh," the boy said. "Sounds pretty crazy."

"Don't play stupid, Teddy."

"I don't know what you're talking about."

"I'm going to say this once," Duncan said. "You have no idea how much shit you are in at the moment. And you better get it through that head of yours that I'm trying to help you."

The boy shook his head.

"You don't get it, Ted—this is just the beginning. Look at your life since this happened. You're falling like a homesick rock. You think that getting off these charges is going to stop that? Two wrongs only make way for more wrongs. You screwed up—you loaded the gun. You can't change that, but you can tell the truth."

"It was Kevin and Bobby," the boy said.

Duncan shook his head. "Yours are the only prints on the bolt," he said. "Kevin's came up on the casing and the trigger and everywhere else, but yours are the only ones on the action of that gun, Ted. They're waiting for a few more test results, but they have what they need to file charges against you."

"No way," he said.

"They've got the physical evidence to corroborate Kevin's story," Duncan said. "What is there to back up yours?"

"My word."

"Pardon me for saying this, Ted, but your word is looking a little shoddy at the moment. And if this little firebomb incident sticks, you're not going to look so repentant."

The boy shook his head. He looked out the window at the tree line. "It was their fault," he said.

"This isn't about them. This is about letting yourself off the hook. You need to understand that. I've seen other boys like you, Ted—boys who never get it and they just keep screwing up and screwing up, just like you're doing now. If you don't come clean, you don't have a chance. I know it."

"I'm not screwing up," he said.

"The day before Bobby was killed you admitted that you and Terry were up here on the Darling property. That day I found the remains of three Molotov cocktails up here in the circle. Last night two very similar incendiary devices were used to light up a car belonging to one of these Young American kids and they're pointing the finger at you, Ted."

"They're just pissed because I stole one of their girl-friends."

"You don't even want to know what they're saying about you and her," Duncan told him.

"I know what they're saying and it's crap. Go ahead and ask Colleen."

"I hope you're right, but you're missing my point, Ted. I'm

not trying to get you in more trouble—I'm trying to keep you out of it. If you just tell the truth, I think we can get you out of most of this mess."

"Take me home," he said.

"For Christ's sake, Ted, we know you loaded the gun. And if you get up there and lie to the judge, it's going to reflect very poorly on you. Lying in court—perjury, Ted. It's a crime. It can be added to whatever else they get you on."

"Take me home."

"I don't have to tell anyone about the broken bottles I found up here, Ted. We can get you off the arson charges. And if you tell us what happened with the Dennisons, I think it'll be clear to everyone that it was just an accident."

"You're lying," he said. "She said you'd do this. I say what you want and then you put me away and they sue us for everything."

"Your mother loves you very much. Too much, Ted. She's not seeing this clearly."

"Take me home now."

"You got to trust me," Duncan told him.

The boy opened the door of the cruiser and pushed himself out. He got his feet under him and sprinted for the tree line, not bothering to close the door of the car. He ran as far and as fast as he could, dodging trees and small saplings, hiking his legs up and over the downed limbs and rocks in his path. When he stopped, his lungs were raw from the fierce breathing. Terry's cigarettes the night before hadn't helped. With his hands on his knees and his head hanging, he heaved several times until the remnants of the egg salad, chips, and cookie poured out his mouth and fell to the dry leaves on the ground.

He hacked and spit several times and wiped his mouth with the sleeve of his sweatshirt. He looked back in the direction of Woodbury Heights and was happy to see that Duncan hadn't followed him.

The floor of the forest was deep with downed leaves and the boy kicked and crashed through them. He jumped a couple of deer as he crested a small knoll. He heard them before he saw them, and then only caught a glimpse of their white tails as they bounded away. On the other side of the knoll, he found the old stone wall he was looking for. If he followed it to the right, he would come to the small creek that eventually crossed the road just down from his house. Instead he turned left on the wall and walked until the stones took a sharp right turn. He knew to bear slightly left from the corner of the wall and walk until he came to the swamp.

When he was young, when trouble had erupted in the house, when his parents had exploded at him or each other, he ran for the woods, where it was quiet and safe. He built small forts and dreamed of never returning. He thought that if he could build a warm enough place to sleep, he could sneak back into his parents' home while they were at work and steal the food and supplies he needed and stay away forever.

The feeling struck him again. He wished he never had to go back to any of it. But even as a child he knew the futility of his escape plans. The evening air poured through the flimsy walls of his small huts and lean-tos. No matter how tightly he thatched the branches that he broke from the surrounding trees, light from the rising moon and stars poured through the makeshift ceilings. The cold and the solitude sent him shivering home every time. Upon his return, he found his parents glued to nighttime television. They looked up, even greeted him, but never seemed to acknowledge his absence. He felt somehow robbed, unable to drum up their attention—they never even acknowledged the familial strife that had sent him running in the first place.

He came to the swamp and walked the edge of it for some time. After fighting through a small stand of young pines, he poked out into his uncle's backyard.

He crossed the small patch of grass and climbed the wooden stairs that led up to the porch. He held a hand to his brow and looked in a window. It wasn't much past noon and he figured his uncle and aunt wouldn't return until five or six. He reached above the light fixture at the top of the door and came down with the spare key. He unlocked the door and returned the key to its hiding place.

The house was quiet and smelled of food. He found some bread and deli meat and made a simple sandwich. He took a box of off-brand cheese-flavored crackers from the top of the refrigerator and poured a small pile of them on the side of his plate. He pulled a beer from the door of the fridge and went to the table to eat. When he finished, he washed and dried his plate, took another beer, drank half, and poured the rest down the drain.

He went into the basement and let himself into his uncle's room. The deer heads stared, wide-eyed and unblinking. The gun cabinets reflected the light that came in from the small cellar windows just below the ceiling. He walked around the room and stopped at the cabinet that held the guns from his house. He pulled at the door but it was locked, so he reached his hand up and ran it along the top of the cabinet. He found the small key and fingered it into the lock.

His father's shotgun was older than the boy but the father had kept it well and the age did not show. There was ornamental carving on the wooden stock and the blue steel receiver of the Remington 1100.

In the years before the Darling land was sold, the father pulled him from school for the first week of deer season—no matter how much his teachers objected. In the woods, on the planks of a tree stand, the father stood with his back to the tree, the boy with his back to the father, the shotgun standing before them both. When the cold finally overtook him, and the boy's body shivered uncontrollably, the father unbuttoned his heavy Woolrich coat, pulled the boy to the warmth inside, and closed the garment around them both—the three, father, son, and firearm, becoming some strange totem.

The boy reached to the floor of the cabinet and fingered open a yellow-and-green box of double-ought buckshot. He let a shell into the chamber. With one hand he released the action, and with the other he let it slowly close. He thumbed the rest of the shells from the box into the belly of the firearm.

He sat in his uncle's chair and stood the gun vertically, stock down, between his knees. He found it difficult to get his top teeth over the front sight. Once past his teeth, the sight dug into the roof of his mouth. When he exhaled, there was a new sound: the hollow call of his breath around the barrel. He closed his eyes and clicked the safety off with his index finger. It was all he could do to focus on the placement of his fingers.

There wasn't room for the guilt, for the sick feelings that over-ran him. There was just enough space for the concentration it took to keep his fingers off the trigger.

He wondered what Lawrence had felt in his final moments behind the barn. For the boy, there was little feeling in it. The concentration it required seemed to quash that part of him. His grandfather's words ricocheted through his head, *Some ways are just no way, some ways are no way, some ways are no way at all.*

The steel of the gun was cold in his damp hands. The smooth wooden stock was slick with his perspiration. He felt guilty for implicating the firearm in such an egregious act, for somehow tainting all the good memories.

He ran his finger along the rounded edge of the trigger guard. The pad of his finger stopped where the guard returned to the stock, where the trigger entered the receiver. His finger slid down in the direction of the floor and found the round button of the safety. He popped it back on.

"Some ways are no way," his whispered when the barrel was free from his mouth. He rested the butt of the stock on his inner thigh and drew back the action. He held out a hand and caught the ejected shell. He closed and opened the action four more times until the magazine was empty.

He took his shirtsleeve and gently wiped the barrel free of the moisture from his breath. He wrapped the cotton around his finger and twisted it inside the muzzle. After he finished with the barrel, he wiped down the receiver and the stock.

With the gun back in the cabinet, he thought how foolish he had been—loading more than one shell, as if one wouldn't have done the trick.

He twisted the lock and pulled the door to his uncle's home closed behind him. He took the porch stairs two at a time and loped across the lawn. Again he fought through the small pines and followed the edge of the swamp. He found the stone wall and walked the length of it. Instead of following the creek to his house, he jumped across it and fought his way up the small hill on the other side. The ground was slick with leaves and he grabbed at small trees to help him up the incline.

Darling's Rock hulked just past the crest of the small knoll. The granite boulder was an oddity in the landscape—it was the size of a small bungalow and sat perched atop the hill. The side he approached was pointed like a shark's snout on one end and slightly rounded on the other, making it look like a distorted map of the United States. He walked up close and rested a hand on the cool, coarse rock. He bent to look into the mouth of a small cavern beneath it—as a child he climbed inside and had immediately felt a wash of terror when he realized the immense weight that hung over him. He'd scampered out and shown his father a souvenir from the cave: a small rounded ball, brown and about the size of a grape or olive.

"It's shit," the father said.

The boy looked closer.

"Porcupine," the father said. "They like places like that."

The boy quickly flung away the turd and wiped his hand on the leg of his dungarees. His father laughed. The boy asked how the rock got there and the father explained glaciers to him—how the huge sheets of ice could move such things at random. The boy tried to imagine it.

"What about the trees?" he asked.

The father passed a flat hand horizontally across the landscape. "No trees."

The boy, now grown and leaning on the rock, tried again to imagine the terrain—nothing but ice, and when it melted, nothing but stone and mud and water in every direction. He walked around the rock, under the overhang of the shark snout, to the flat face of the far side. Names and dates were chiseled into the stone, the oldest going back to the 1700s, when the surrounding area was most likely nothing but pasture—having been logged barren again.

What little he knew of his family history told him they had not yet arrived in the area at that time. They were French-Canadians who had fought in the Civil War in exchange for American citizenship. Even after fighting for the Union, the early French immigrants were ostracized by the town. They were forbidden to attend the local Catholic church, and so built their own—St. Peter's, the parish the boy's family still attended when holidays brought them around to mass.

He turned from the rock and looked out into the forest. He realized that his family was not unlike the folks who now populated the new developments. They came, clung close to one another, and bore the brunt of the locals' condemnation. Their acceptance required time, and more than that, another new group to persecute. For the first time, he saw a fundamental flaw in the Youth doctrine—they fought to preserve a status quo where there had never been anything but change.

He left Darling's Rock and followed the ridge up and around until he saw the open backyards of Sandy Creek. He quickly jogged between two houses to the street. From the edge of the pavement, he followed the brick walkway up to the front steps of the house. He looked at the chandelier and walked to the door. He reached out and touched the glowing doorbell. He heard the chime inside and he heard footsteps approaching. The door opened and Mrs. Dennison stood in front of him. She didn't flinch. She didn't cry out or fly into a fit of rage. Mrs. Dennison stood in the open door and looked at him. She was dressed in a pair of jeans and a blue sweat-shirt. She didn't look mad or sad or much of anything.

"Theodore," she said.

"Mrs. Dennison." He looked at her feet. She had on white leather sneakers.

"Kevin's at school," she told him.

"I know," he said.

"Why aren't you at school?"

"I didn't feel good."

"Are you feeling better now?"

He shook his head.

"Do you have a cold?" she said. "The flu?"

"I'm awful hung-over," he said. He looked up at her and she nodded.

"Kevin's been drinking and smoking marijuana something terrible," she said. "We don't know what to do."

He nodded.

"I can't say I blame him," she said. "If I thought it would help, I'd do it too."

"It doesn't," he said.

"I know. I'd ask you inside but the house is a mess. I haven't had the energy for that sort of thing. You want to sit?" She stepped out of the house and motioned to the steps. He turned and took a seat on the second step from the top. She sat

on the step above his, on the opposite side. "Thank goodness
we have someone to take care of the yard," she said. They
looked out at the lawn, the shaped shrubs, the small mulched
island planted with a variety of small flowers. They sat for a
moment without speaking.

"I loaded the gun," he said.

"I know you did," she said.

He looked down at his hands. "I'm sorry."

"I know," she said. "There was a time when I hated you for
it, but I'm through that."

He nodded.

"Did you ever hate me?" she said.

He shrugged.

"You can say it. It's okay."

"I did," he said.

"It felt good, didn't it? Better, anyway. It felt better."

"Anything felt better," he said.

"I thought I'd have to kill myself to get away from it. I had
to see someone. I have to take pills."

He reached down and pulled back the sleeve of his sweatshirt. He pushed the cuff up past his forearm to his elbow. He
rotated his arm so that the inside pointed toward the sky. A
scabbed, smiling face stood out against the pale flesh. He
looked from Mrs. Dennison down to his arm and pointed to
the burn with his index finger.

"What's that?" she said.

"Burn."

"From what?"

"Top of a lighter."

"You did it?"

He nodded.

"Did it feel good?"

"It felt really good."

"You shouldn't," she said. "Not anymore. That wouldn't make Bobby happy. He wouldn't want that."

Tears poked out of the corners of his eyes and crawled down his cheeks. "I'm so goddamn sorry." His chin bounced as he spoke.

"I know, honey." Her voice cracked. She reached over and rubbed his back. She slid closer and put an arm around his shoulder. Their bodies shook together.

He wiped at his eyes with a sleeve. "I'm going to tell what happened," he said.

"That's good."

"Please don't sue us," he said.

"What?"

"Don't sue my parents, please."

"You don't have anything I want," she told him. "It wouldn't bring him back."

He looked out at the lawn.

"I don't think about him as much as I used to," she said. "Sometimes I feel like a bad mother because of that. I feel so terrible letting him go. But I try to think of what he would want. First I thought he wanted me to vindicate him or something. But that's what I wanted. He just wants us to be happy."

"I hope so," he said.

"He's forgiven you," she said. "I know he has."

"Kevin probably hates me," he said.

Mrs. Dennison shrugged. "At the moment it's easier for me to communicate with the dead than the living."

"I bet he's pissed," he said.

"He's a lot like us. He's so busy being mad at everyone else, he can't see how mad he is at himself."

"I'm not mad."

"Look at your arm again and tell me that," she said. "You've got to let it go."

"I don't know how."

"Yes you do." She smiled at him. "You do. You're doing it right now."

From Sandy Creek the boy walked back in the direction of his house. As he walked down the side of the road, his bus roared past. The wake of the vehicle gusted and seemed to push him off balance. He stepped into the sand on the side of the road and regained his footing. Before he got to the Humphreys', he kicked around in the downed leaves on the side of the road in search of a few suitable stones. He came up with one about the size of a baseball, worn smooth and oblong like an egg. A few feet over he found a smaller, more jagged one. He gripped the smoother piece of granite in his throwing hand and held the smaller one on the opposite side for backup. He crossed the road to put the tarmac between him and the Humphreys' yard.

He saw the dog lying at the top of the drive, next to the cargo van that hadn't moved in years. The dog's head rested on the pavement between its two outstretched paws. The boy was halfway past the yard when the dog's ears perked up and its head rose. It scrambled to its feet and trotted down the drive and across the yard. A low rumble came from the dog. Its long fur hung in patches of white, black, and several shades of brown. The boy knew he shouldn't make eye contact with the dog, but he did. He half hoped the dog would come for him, would cross the pavement and make a lunge. He wanted an excuse to club it with the rock. He held it up and ready. The dog came a few feet out onto the pavement and barked once, sharp and loud. It snarled at him and its jaws popped. The boy didn't turn his back to it, but he kept walking. He kept the rock ready. The dog made several false lunges at him, but it seemed to understand the threat of the raised stone. It didn't come within striking distance.

It followed him well past the Humphreys' property line. The boy grew tired of walking backward, but anytime he tried to turn around, the dog made for his heels.

"Go on," he shouted. "Git!" But the dog still slunk along on the opposite side of the street. He swapped the two stones in his hands. He got a good grip on the small jagged rock. He turned his back to the dog but kept an eye over his shoulder. The dog came for him. He waited until it was well into the road. When the dog was close, he turned, hopped twice quickly, and overhanded the stone. It caught the dog in the rib cage with a hollow, dull sound. The dog shuddered at the blow and let out a quick yelp. It cowered for a moment in the middle of the road before turning to skulk away. When he saw the dog turn, he burst into a sprint after it, letting his feet fall hard and loud on the tarmac. The dog shot a quick glance back at him and bolted into the woods. He watched until the dog was out of sight.

He heard a car coming. He saw that he was in the middle of the road and took several quick steps to the opposite ditch. The noise grew as the car approached. It came around the bend ahead of him and he was glad that he still had the larger of the two stones. Jason Becker's Volkswagen slowed and pulled off the road just ahead of him. He thought about ducking into the woods and making a run for it, but he was tired of all that. He was surprised to see that only Jason, George, and Peckerhead were in the car. They climbed out and walked toward him. Jason and George were in the front. Peckerhead lingered back, near the hood of the car.

"You can put the rock down, Theodore," George said. "We're not here for anything like that."

"It's not for you," he said.

"You can put it down," George told him.

He shook his head.

"You're a coward," Becker said.

"Jason," George said, "you said you could do this."

"This little punk sets my car on fire and you want me to be cordial? Fuck that," Becker said. "Don't even try to deny it."

"I won't," said the boy. "Long as you don't try to deny tearing up my yard."

"Only because you raped Colleen, you fuck," Jason said.

"You know it wasn't like that," the boy said. "Peckerhead, tell him, for Christ's sake."

Peckerhead shrugged. He stayed back by the car.

"Guys," George said. "We can go back and forth like this forever. And where will it get us? Nowhere. So just quit it for a minute. Please." He looked at both Jason and the boy. "This is exactly what they want. It's infighting. It distracts us and weakens our cause. I've been thinking, and as it stands I'd say we're all about even. I think we can call it water under the bridge and get on with business."

"You want him back?" Becker said.

"Not immediately," George said.

"You're kidding me," Becker said. "He rapes your girl-friend and torches my car and you want him back?"

"I didn't rape her, you idiot," the boy told Becker. "She wanted it and you know it."

"What did you call me?" Becker said.

"A dumb-ass," he said.

Becker came at him. The boy had the rock back and ready, but George jumped between the two and got a palm on both of their chests.

"What is wrong with you two?" George hollered.

Jason swatted at George's hand and tried to push him out of the way.

The boy pushed George's hand off of him, but rather than stepping away, he took a step closer. George was busy with Jason and he never saw the blow coming. The rock landed on the side of his head, just above his ear, just where the boy had aimed. It sounded like a stick coming down quickly on a wet sack of mud. George's head bucked at the impact and he went to the ground like liquid. His face landed in the sand and his arms sprawled at odd angles from his torso. His eyes stared blankly at the far side of the street. His pupils twitched back and forth so fast they seemed to vibrate. Sand clung to his cheek and his body shivered. His hair was already wet around the wound. For a moment, it was quiet. The boy couldn't say why he did it, but even in the act of protecting him, George seemed more threatening than Jason could ever have been.

"What the fuck," Jason said to the boy.

He stepped back and held the rock up and ready.

"What is wrong with you?" Jason said. He looked back to

George and squatted down beside him. "George? Man, you all right?" George didn't respond. Peckerhead came close and looked down. Jason looked up at him. "Get help," he said. "Go."

Peckerhead looked at the boy.

"My house is closest," he said. "Come on." He broke into a run and he heard Peckerhead calling after him.

"I think you killed him," Peckerhead said.

He didn't answer. He turned into his driveway and then down the sidewalk. He ran up the stairs and found the door locked. He jabbed at the doorbell until he heard the lock turn in the door. He pushed through the door and by his mother and went to the telephone.

"You have got some explaining to do," she said.

He dialed the three numbers and waited. He told the dispatch that a boy was unconscious on the side of the road and he gave her a general location.

"Was there an accident?" the dispatcher said.

"No," he told her. "I hit him." There was a pause. "You should probably send the police too," he said.

His mother had him by the arm. "What is going on?"

He hung up the phone. "I hit George Haney," he said. He held up the stone for his mother to see. "He's out on the side of the road. He might be dead."

His mother stared at him.

"I'm going to tell them the truth," he said. "I already told Mrs. Dennison."

She reached back and slapped him across the face. It stung but he didn't move. He looked her in the eye. She took a breath like she was about to let him have it, but she stopped.

"Fine," she said. "But you're on your own. All of it," she swung a hand toward the front door. "It's yours." She turned and walked down the hall. She grabbed the railing and began climbing the stairs. He heard the door of her bedroom close.

He walked back outside. He followed the sidewalk and the driveway back out to the street. Jason squatted on his haunches next to George. He was bare-chested and he held what must have been his shirt to the side of George's head. Peckerhead stood above the two with his hand on the hood of the Volkswagen. He looked at the boy for a moment but then looked back to George.

The boy walked back to his driveway and sat on the edge of the stone wall. He heard the sirens approaching and he watched the ambulance blow past. Shortly after, the local cruiser passed. He knew it wouldn't be long.

He stood when the cruiser pulled in. Duncan looked at him, leaned down, and said something into the radio. He opened the door and stepped out. He came around the front of the car and stood before the boy.

"Can't say I didn't warn you," Duncan said.

"Is he dead?"

Duncan smiled and shook his head.

The boy nodded. "How bad?"

"Pretty mean concussion," Duncan said. "Some stitches and rest and he'll be fine."

"I was afraid I killed him," he said.

Duncan shook his head and smiled. "Nah, just knocked the heck out of him."

The boy shrugged.

"So what's your story," Duncan said. "I got three guys over there saying you just blindsided him."

"That sounds about right."

"Was he threatening you?" Duncan asked. "Talking like he was going to hurt you or anything?"

"No," he said.

"Ted," Duncan said, "you're not giving me much to work with."

"You going to take me in?"

"I'm afraid I'm going to have to."

"Will you get that trooper?" he said. "Thompson?"

"How come?"

"'Cause I want to talk to him."

"Sure," Duncan said. "We can make that happen."

"You going to cuff me?"

"Nah. Just get in." Duncan opened the front door and the boy climbed inside. He pulled the door shut and drew the seat belt across his chest. Duncan stood outside for a moment, talking into his radio. He climbed in and they backed out.

As they drive, the boy stares out the window at the blur of the forest. The car feels like a bubble, the windows bulging out against the world. He knows that outside, it's all still happening. And once he steps out of the cruiser, it will begin again. He wishes for even a week, a month, or a year more, but there isn't any more time. Nothing will stop.

His face is reflected in the window at his side and he looks through himself to see the world outside. The next economic boom is already beginning out there, wherever that sort of thing happens. The forest outside the window will be cut for new house lots and condominium developments. The town will sing again with chainsaws—the pop of nail guns providing a disjointed rhythm for the sickly wail of power tools. One day he will look at the same road and hardly be able to see the world where all of this transpired. There will be glints of it here and there—a place where the old faded tarmac peeks out from under the new pavement, the house of an elderly couple that resists renovation—but for the most part, it will disappear, it will change, and all the while, his own memory of it will recede farther and farther from him.

He sits on the corner of his bed and with the tip of his finger he traces the ornamental engraving on the wooden stock and steel receiver. He rolls the gun upright and with the butt on his thigh he reaches up and opens the action. The sound of sliding metal and the clack of the action locking in place break the silence in the room. Holding the lever firm, he thrusts the bolt forward and closed again. He pulls the gun to his shoulder and looks down the sights, taking aim on a model airplane that hangs from the ceiling. Then he quickly slings the barrel to the side, bearing down on a ceramic figurine.

It's a pink piggy bank, and it seems to point out a certain absurdity. The gun has gone the way of the dirt bikes and four-wheel-drive trucks—now that the roads have been paved and the sand pits landscaped. It's difficult for him to think that he will never again hunt the hill behind his house. He looks at the .22, and it's still difficult to think that he will never again see Bobby Dennison.

Telling the truth about loading the gun wasn't quite the cure-all that he'd hoped it would be. With the stories corroborated and clear on paper, Trooper Thompson and the attorney general did agree that the shooting was indeed accidental and that Kevin and Theodore had suffered enough. But that wasn't the end of their legal troubles. Kevin was recently arrested on a possession charge when he was pulled over with marijuana in his pocket. The boy was charged with assault for what he did to George. Duncan assured him that mandatory counseling would be included in his sentence.

The boy takes a slow breath and runs his fingers along the inside of his arm. He pulls up the sleeve of his shirt to look. He traces the wicked smiles with the tip of a finger. Some of the older scars have faded slightly, melting back into his skin, forming soft, pale outlines in his flesh. While he can't give it up, the burns blossom less frequently.

He lets the sleeve of his shirt fall and he takes the .22 and slides it back under his bed. He hopes to give it to some child of his at an appropriate moment, and though it feels strange, he hopes the child will in turn do the same. It isn't so much the desire to possess the gun itself, but rather the ill feeling that comes over him when he thinks of someone else taking it up, perhaps with no idea of what it has done.

Acknowledgments

The author wishes to thank the Syracuse University Creative Writing Program, the Western Michigan University Prague Summer Program in Creative Writing, and the Summer Literary Seminars in St. Petersburg for their support; Peter Straus, Melanie Jackson, Daniel Menaker, and the gang at Random House for their belief in this manuscript; Arthur Flowers and George Saunders for their kindness and wisdom from the beginning to the end of this project; Mary Karr for revealing an easier, softer way through it all; the following technical advisers: Chris Decker, firearms instructor and armorer for the New Hampshire State Police, Wendy Foley of the Windham, New Hampshire, Police Department, Kenneth R. Martell of the Bristol, New Hampshire, Police Department, Phillip

Maurice LaMarche of the Plattsburgh, New York, Fire Department; and the following readers for their advice and encouragement: Christian TeBordo, Adam Levin, Nina Shope, Erin Brooks Worley, Rahul Mehta, Stephanie Carpenter, Brian Evenson, Tobias Wolff, Robert Eversz, and Michael Schellenberg.

The author would also like to thank his family, Patty and Todd Davis, for their understanding and support; Cheryl and Greg Doble for sharing their home and their two wonderful boys; his parents for all the slingshots, guns, fireworks, and dirt bikes, for sticking by him through the ensuing trips to the hospital, for the hunting and fishing, and for showing him all the fun and beauty there is to be had in the world. He would also like to express his gratitude to Caroline, his best friend, his partner in crime, his favorite.

ABOUT THE AUTHOR

PHIL LaMARCHE was a writing fellow in the Syracuse University graduate creative writing program. He was also awarded the Ivan Klíma Fellowship in fiction in Prague and a Summer Literary Seminars fellowship in St. Petersburg, Russia. His story "In the Tradition of My Family," published in the spring 2005 edition of *Ninth Letter* and the *2005 Robert Olen Butler Prize Stories* anthology, has been made into a film by orLater Productions. He lives in central New York State.

ABOUT THE TYPE

This book was set in Sabon, a typeface
designed by the well-known German ty-
pographer Jan Tschichold (1902–74).
Sabon's design is based upon the origi-
nal letter forms of Claude Garamond
and was created specifically to be used
for three sources: foundry type for hand
composition, Linotype, and Monotype.
Tschichold named his typeface for the
famous Frankfurt typefounder Jacques
Sabon, who died in 1580.